Helen Ekin Starrett

Letters to Elder Daughters

Married and unmarried

Helen Ekin Starrett

Letters to Elder Daughters
Married and unmarried

ISBN/EAN: 9783743407657

Manufactured in Europe, USA, Canada, Australia, Japa

Cover: Foto ©Andreas Hilbeck / pixelio.de

Manufactured and distributed by brebook publishing software (www.brebook.com)

Helen Ekin Starrett

Letters to Elder Daughters

TO

ELDER DAUGHTERS

MARRIED AND UNMARRIED

BY

HELEN EKIN STARRETT

AUTHOR OF "LETTERS TO A DAUGHTER," "FUTURE
OF EDUCATED WOMEN," ETC.

CHICAGO
A. C. McCLURG AND COMPANY
1888

By A. C. McClurg and Company
A. D. 1887

CONTENTS.

LETTERS

TO

ELDER DAUGHTERS.

———◆———

THE IDEAL FAMILY.

A FAMOUS English thinker and writer, W. R. Greg, once wrote an interesting essay entitled " Unrealizable Ideals." In enumerating these he did not include the ideal family ; and yet it is probable that there is no ideal so generally or so fondly cherished and so seldom realized. The young couple joining hearts and hands and efforts in their intention to build a home almost always have a high ideal of what that home shall be, and fondly believe that never into their charmed circle shall come those differences and indifferences, and irritabilities and selfishnesses, which they have seen in other homes, which have taken all the romance, bloom, and freshness out of family life, and have left it too often a dull routine of joyless drudgery, — a prosaic, uninteresting fact.

Probably one of the fundamental difficulties in the way of realizing a high ideal of home and family life lies in the fact that too much importance is given in that ideal to the happiness or pleasure to be enjoyed, and too little to the duties to be performed. In imagination the young couple see themselves seated around the ideal table, partaking of the ideal food. They give little thought to the labor and care for both husband and wife that must precede the regular furnishing forth of that table.

To realize the ideal family board usually means, for the husband, unending days of labor and business anxiety; for the wife, constant attention to the prosaic details of kitchen and pantry and laundry. That ideal bread will not make itself, and very few of those who propose to serve us in our kitchens can make it. That ambrosial coffee, that nicely broiled steak, that delicate dessert, are all the product of work.

That shining-smooth table-cloth and those satin-smooth napkins will not come out of any unsuperintended laundry. Let no one expect to realize the ideal who is not willing to accept the conditions necessary to its realization. God hath set the one over against the other, and they are inseparable.

This, however, is merely an illustration of a great underlying general principle. The ideal table is a pleasant and desirable concomitant of the ideal home, but it is, in comparison with many other things, of comparatively small importance. The first great essentials of the ideal home and the ideal family are constant love, confidence, devotion, unselfishness, willingness to spend and be spent in the service of one another. The ideal home is one where the children shall say: "When we marry and have homes of our own, we wish to love and be loved as our father and mother love each other." It is where the sons are taught respect for all women by the deference and kindness of their father to their mother; it is where daughters learn from their mother's patient example how beautiful a thing wifely and motherly affection is, — learn the beauty of daily unselfish devotion to the good of all. It is one where the atmosphere of love and kindness is so all-pervading that it softens every privation, ennobles every humble duty, and stimulates constantly all noble and unselfish aims.

This ideal can never be attained where there is not a fairly equal reciprocity in devotion, labor, and self-denial, between the different members of the family. Here is the rock on which many a family is wrecked after it has had a propitious launching. It is possible for devotion on the part of one to breed selfishness on the part of another. Sometimes it is the wife whose every wish and need is anticipated by the devoted husband, who learns to take for granted all this attention and love, without realizing any particular need for reciprocity of duty and affection on her part, and who, in consequence, develops a selfishness and helplessness that will inevitably, in future years, mar the best home life. Sometimes it is the husband, taking for granted the affectionate attentions and labors of his wife, accepting at her hands services and sacrifices entirely out of proportion to her share of matrimonial duties, who becomes in the end exacting, imperious, and tyrannical. Sometimes — nay, oftenest of all — it is the children who absorb the time, attention, and deference of their parents to a degree that develops them into little tyrants; reverses the law of parental rule, and makes everything and every person about the home subservient to their undisciplined tempers and immature desires.

These dangers beset the home and family in its earlier development. Passing on to the period when children are approaching maturity, other dangers and perplexities arise. It becomes a problem with parents, as their children approach mature years, how much restraint or surveillance shall be exercised over their outgoings and incomings and conduct generally. Happy they whose children desire in all these things to have the approbation of their parents, and who have nothing to conceal in conduct or associations. But, however this may be, one thing is certain, — that a reasonable amount of freedom must be granted to the young people in the home. Constant surveillance is something which no intelligent person, young or old, can endure with equanimity. We can all of us recall to mind homes where no member of the family could have any little secret or plan or preference without being beset by other members of the family, or by parents, for explanation; where no member could bring in a favorite playmate or companion, or carry on a favorite correspondence, without arousing a kind of jealousy on the part of the others; where no one could indulge any little idiosyncrasy in regard to dress or food without being guyed by the others and rendered unhappy by irritating criticisms. Perfect freedom for all members of the family within the limits of home life is one of the essential elements in every ideal family.

Nor can any home be an ideal home where the interests or convenience or preferences of any member of the family obtain an undue ascendency, or selfishly control the actions of the rest. Who has not seen the home where everything in the way of comfort depended upon keeping the father or the mother in good temper, and where the accidental annoying or displeasing of either enveloped the whole house in an atmosphere of discomfort; where the disarrangement of the hours for meals by the unexpected arrival of guests, or by some change in household arrangement necessary for their accommodation, is accompanied by black looks, irritating expressions, and even downright rudeness? And who cannot recall that pitiable sight of a wife or a husband struggling to maintain outward composure and to present a smiling and welcoming face while trying to conceal or divert attention from the irritation and bad manners of the other?

In many a family one person may have the power to make all the rest so uncomfortable by irritability and crossness, if his or her wishes are not obeyed, that, merely to escape this discomfort, the rest will hasten to accede to anything demanded. This is a temper which, if it is seen developing in children, should be resisted with the greatest firmness by the parents. (Alas, if it is one of the parents in whom it develops!) Sometimes it is an elder son who, because he is in college, is looked up to by the other children, who will demand from them a subservience to his wishes that is humiliating to them and hurtful to him. Sometimes it is the daughter just beginning to go into society, who suddenly becomes selfishly important and is tempted to domineer over the younger and other members of the family. Such a disposition must be checked in its incipiency with a strong hand, or it may become an element of permanent discord and unhappiness in the home.

Nowhere are beautiful manners so beautiful as in the home, especially when they are not put on merely for company, but are an integral part of every-day conduct. The conservators of manners in the home are usually the mothers and daughters; for men and boys, in their rough-and-tumble contact with business life, are apt to acquire brusque, imperious ways, and a harshness of speech that often pains and wounds. The quick recognition and enjoyment by the public of the exaggerated portraiture of the Spoopendyke papers was due to the fact that in most families where there are men and boys there is apt to be considerable Spoopendyke talk. It is a kind of talk that, if unchecked, will ultimately spoil all the fine bloom of family affectionateness. So, too, there is often on the part of growing boys an indifference and disregard of those minor rules of behavior at table and elsewhere that tend to mar the fine ideal of home life. To eliminate all these "little foxes that spoil the vines" is especially the task and care of the mother, in which, however, she should be assisted both by the precept and the example of the father. It is a work that requires infinite patience. It is not accomplished in a month, or in a year, or in ten years. It is not completed till every child has come to the full measure and stature of manhood and womanhood after the model of Christ and his teachings. But no higher aim can be set before any young couple starting out in life than the noble one of rearing an ideal family.

YOUNG WIFE AS HOUSEKEEPER.

THE sensible mother of several fine, ambitious, and industrious sons, all of whom seemed on the high-road to business and social success, was congratulated by a friend upon the probability that their future was happily assured, their characters formed, and their principles rightly established. To which the mother replied: "I have as yet one great solicitude for them, and that is for their possible marriage; for, looking around and thinking over the young girls I know, I can think of but one in all my circle of acquaintances who, in my opinion, would make a good wife for a young man who has his own way to make in life; and a wife nearly always makes or mars a young man's future."

On being pressed for the reason of her fears for the young girls of to-day, this mother said: "There is a lack of both

physical and mental stamina in the younger
generation of girls that is quite distressing
when we consider the responsibilities that
are sure to be laid upon them if they
marry. In the first place, they are not
industrious in the right way. The most
of them are constantly busy about some
whim or other ; but generally it is about
something ephemeral, something that produces a pleasurable temporary excitement,
after which they experience a reaction that
neutralizes all possible good effects of their
activity. For instance, a young girl will
work enthusiastically in preparing for a
camping or boating excursion, will prove
herself very ˙capable and skilful in the
preparation of food for such an excursion ;
yet by no possibility can that skill and
industry be made available in keeping the
house in order or improving the family
table. Oh, no! that is too humdrum!
There is no fun in that! Another young
girl will display extraordinary taste and
ingenuity in devising and making a party
dress, possibly from worn or unpromis-
ing materials, but her every-day wearing-

apparel may show in every garment want
of care and neatness. There is lack of a
spirit of steady industry, of definite aim,
of any sense of responsibility beyond that
of merely getting through with whatever
work must be done. This work is regarded
as something disagreeable, to be hurried
through with as a matter of no special interest. Now, when such young girls marry
what is generally their ideal of home life ?
Is it of a partnership in which they shall
bravely bear their share of labor and responsibility and self-denial, if need be ?
By no means. It is of an establishment
which shall spring ready-furnished from
the hands of furniture-makers and uphol-
sterers; where servants, paid out of the
husband's perhaps slender income, shall do
all the work, take all the petty care, and
leave them free as before to have a good
time. All the heavy burden of responsibility for the keeping up and running of
the establishment is to fall on the head
and shoulders of the young husband. To
marry in these days is a dangerous risk for
any young man."

To all of which it might be replied, first, that it is not wholly the fault of the young girls of to-day that they are not better prepared for the responsibilities of wifehood. Too many things are, in these days, pressed upon the attention of young girls, — too many studies, too many diversions, too much going about, too much of seeing people. If they have failed to form habits of steady industry in the home, or to learn the various household arts that are so essential to the comfort of a home, it may be, nay, often is, because they have never been rightly set to work by their mothers, nor afforded a fair opportunity to learn and practise these household arts. Nearly all households are suffering to-day from over-pressure of some kind or other that prevents mothers from giving that care to the training of their daughters in habits of industry or in knowledge of household arts which all young girls should receive. To make up for deficiencies in these directions the young wife needs, above all things, to be guided by a high sense of duty, and by a sincere, unselfish determination to do

2

her share in the work of building up a home.

We live in a time of change and confusion in all matters pertaining to the domestic arrangements of our homes. Social life makes demands upon us that seem to require the delegating of a very considerable part of the domestic work of our homes to servants. But most young wives err in delegating too much and expecting too much. If a young wife has not had the opportunity to learn all domestic arts before her marriage, what a capital chance she has in the home all her own to do so! Right here is the first opportunity of the young wife, and the first demand upon her for unselfish industry. She should begin at once to look well to the ways of her household. She should be astir in the early morning hours. Late rising is the bane both of domestic order and of health. It is not possible to impress this fact too strongly upon the young wife. Show me the household where the wife and mother is an habitually late riser, and I will show you one where disorder, lack of promptness, carelessness on the part of servants, and general household discomfort prevail. It is no sign whatever that one should be in bed late because one feels indisposed to rise and begin the activities of the day. It may indicate that one should go to bed earlier, or that a short after-dinner nap would be a good thing; but no increase of vital energy was ever gained by late sleeping in the morning. No; the young wife should be up and around, and especially should she be on hand to see that the most important meal of the day is prepared of wholesome materials in a wholesome manner. As an interested observer of the ways of young married people lately remarked: "Many a young man goes to his business wholly unfitted for the work of the day by the quality of the food he has eaten for his breakfast."

It seems like the repetition of a worn-out theme to urge upon the young wife the importance of thoroughly understanding the art of the right preparation of food. And yet it cannot be too often reiterated or too greatly emphasized. There has been

too much of a disposition in late years
among young women to underestimate this
department of a wife's duties. They smile
scornfully and say they despise the old
adage that " the way to a man's heart is
through his stomach." It may not be the
way to his heart, but it is certainly one of
the bonds to draw a man constantly to his
home, that he shall find there a pleasant
and appetizing home table and loving attention to his comfort even in the material
needs of his life. The young wife needs to
remember, too, that all day long her husband labors to bring to his home those
material things which are necessary to its
existence. Modern business life is hard
work and an intense strain both upon the
mental and physical powers, and she is
unworthy the name of wife who will not
practise a fairly corresponsive industry in
the home.

But there is another reason why it is
better for a young wife to be industriously
active about her home, which is this : nothing is so conducive to health. After all the
evolutions of the gymnasiums and inven-

tions of calisthenic movements for young women in schools, no such healthful exercise has ever been invented as ordinary household work. How have sensible people smiled to themselves at the various movements invented by movement-cure physicians, and others, as they have recognized in them exercises similar to those of going up or down stairs, or handling the broom, or moving furniture! If ordinary household work greatly fatigues any ordinary young woman, it is only a sign that she has flabby, undeveloped muscles, and needs to call to her aid a little spunk and energy. If she will practise such work a reasonable amount of time every day with spirit and cheerfulness, she will inevitably reap the reward of an invigorated body.

I emphasize this material side of the duty of a young wife because I am deeply convinced that this indisposition to bodily activity on her part is one of the great dangers in the young homes springing up all over our land, and one of the main causes of ill health in young women. Physicians are to blame in that they are too ready to advise against any kind of bodily exercise that is of the nature of work. The truth is that one good sweeping of an ordinary parlor is worth a dozen carriage rides as healthful exercise for a normally constituted young woman. It will bring the color to her cheeks and send the blood coursing through her veins as scarcely any other exercise will. If it tires her she should practise it till it does not tire her.

It will, however, depend wholly upon circumstances whether sweeping the parlor should be any part of a young wife's duties; but the active superintendence of her house can never be otherwise than her duty if she is physically able to perform the work. The making of a home and the active superintendence of it are the duties that most of all dignify young wifehood. The practice of many young people, of beginning married life in a boarding-house or hotel, is a pitiable mistake. It cuts the young wife off from all opportunity for the exercise of those faculties and virtues which make home life rich. Worthy occupation of our powers and faculties is one of the necessary conditions of happiness; and to see an intelligent young woman spending the long hours while her husband is at work, in comparative idleness, or in devising plans to amuse herself, or in some trifling occupation that brings no worthy result, impresses every thoughtful observer as being an abnormal and wrong state of things. By all means let the young couple go to housekeeping, if it is only in two or three rooms with an oil-stove and a table hinged against the wall. It will make the young husband a better husband; it will make the young wife a better wife.

YOUNG WIFE AS HOMEKEEPER.

HOUSEKEEPING and homekeeping are two very different things. There is many a well-kept house that has scarcely an element of the true home. There are many beloved and cherished homes where there is not very good housekeeping. Housekeeping under certain circumstances may be slighted, and there are times when it becomes the housekeeper's duty, for the sake of other duties, to make her housekeeping secondary, — but the homekeeping, never. "Do you keep house and take care of your children?" asked one young mother of another. "No; I take care of my children and keep house," was the sensible reply. To proportion rightly the work and care of a home between housekeeping and homekeeping requires an amount of wisdom and patience such as no one who has not tried it can estimate. Great are the responsibili-

ties of the young wife; perplexing and discouraging the problems which will continually arise in the complex home life of
to-day. She will need, above all things,
patience and the ever-sustaining power of
a deep sense of duty. These are the foundation stones of the home where love will
live and grow and become stronger and
more precious with every passing year.

There is a common fact to which nearly
every young wife must reconcile her mind
at an early period in her married life, and
that is that the cares of the home, with
all their multiplicity and wearisomeness of
detail, will devolve chiefly upon her. Her
husband will be mainly absorbed in his business, if he is a good business man. The pe-
culiarity of the business life of to-day is
the strain it puts on the attention during
business hours, so that everything foreign
to it is almost necessarily excluded. So the
young housekeeper must not be disappoint-
ed and become piqued and pouty if John
shows a decided reluctance to attend to any
small matters pertaining to the household.
I have known a young wife to make herself

unhappy for days over the circumstance of her husband declaring, somewhat emphatically, that he could not take time to stop at the grocer's on his way to business to order soap and starch on Monday morning. She said to herself, and finally said to him, that before their marriage he could spend an hour at any time in rushing all over town to match a shade of embroidery silk or find a certain kind of rose for her to wear to a party. Why this change, unless he was ceasing to care for her wishes and convenience? All such exaggerated sensitiveness needs to be put aside by firm good sense. In married life, as in all other relations of the home, a great deal must be taken for granted. To be constantly on the watch for little lapses and failures in attention is like pulling the earth away from planted seeds in order to see if they are growing. Not but that little attentions should be lovingly continued and the tender plant of love constantly and tenderly cherished; but there should be no suspicion or reproaches for little inattentions or omissions that may merely be the result of absorption in cares and the necessary work of life. The best way for a young wife to secure loving attention from her husband is to hold his love by her gentle and steadfast kindness and faithfulness, and his admiration and respect by the manner in which she fulfils the duties that fall to her share in the domestic partnership. This she will utterly fail in doing if she becomes querulous, fault-finding, suspicious, or undertakes to keep calling him to account on unimportant matters in connection with their home life.

It has often been objected, of late years, that entirely too much stress has been laid upon the wife's duties in the home, and too little on the husband's. There is much truth in this, and it is also true that a great deal more ought to be written and spoken (and read) about the duties of husbands. But these thoughts are addressed especially to young wives, and it is their duties we are considering. They are the ones to whom a broad knowledge of human nature, and especially of man-nature, is most valuable. Hence it is always harder for a young wife who has been brought up in a family without boys to adjust herself to her new relations. She has had no opportunity to observe the development of the boy into the man, and hence cannot so easily understand that boyish selfishnesses and crudities often linger along even after the boy has entered on a really noble manhood. There can be no doubt that young women mature mentally and morally much earlier than young men; so that a wife of twenty may be more mature and well-balanced in mind and disposition than the husband of twenty-six or seven. Young men are often like fruits that ripen late, and we are obliged to be patient with them until life with its responsibilities, and especially until the development of the family affections, mellows and sweetens and softens them. To have this patience is especially the duty that falls to the young wife. If she have it not, the probable result will be bickerings and quarrels which will in time utterly destroy the dignity of the home and of married life. Of this fact the details of evidence in divorce courts give emphatic proof, as many of the stories told there simply reveal both husband and wife quarrelling, criminating, recriminating, calling names, and oftentimes even striking each other like a couple of undisciplined children.

Remembering that good temper and the careful avoidance of bickerings of all kinds are the first essentials of a happy home life, the consideration of other special home duties follows easily and happily. The atmosphere of the home will be mainly determined by the wife, as also will its relation to the world and society. She will have, what probably her husband will not have, leisure for reading, for the cultivation of her tastes in music, literature, or art, and she should carefully improve such opportunities. It may be her beautiful work to prevent her husband from becoming wholly absorbed in the material cares of life; to prevent him from wasting all his evenings over the heterogeneous, innutritious, sapless literature of the daily papers, which she can only do by interesting him in something better. She may make music or art interesting to him by her own constant progress and interest in them. She it is who will largely determine the character of the friends who shall visit at the home. If by her good sense and intelligence and cheerful hospitality she can attract and secure the society of the good and intelligent, she will have won priceless treasures for the young home of whose happiness she is so largely the conservator, and thrown a safeguard around her husband which will be second in its power for good only to her own hold on his respect and affections. To accomplish all this is surely an aim worthy a young woman's highest ambition.

THE MOTHER AT HOME.

THE mother is the heart of the home. She it is who determines its characteristics and diffuses through it that subtle atmosphere which every sensitive person can feel when introduced into the home circle, and from which can quickly be inferred the ruling spirit of the home. It makes no difference whether it be the home of wealth or of poverty; whether the mother be a woman of education or comparatively unlettered; that which determines the mother's place in it transcends schools and circumstances. It is the spiritual plane on which she lives, it is the motives which influence her life, that determine her influence and measure her power in moulding the character of her children. That which will place the mother in the highest relation in the home is the conviction, on the part of her children, that unselfish love for them and a desire to do right towards them and others will always guide her actions; that their mother may be depended upon for justice and generosity and truth and kindness toward every one. She will love her children with deep devotion and yet not wholly selfishly. Her mother-heart can take in the needs of children who are not hers, and devise kind and loving things for them. What lesson in kindness and care for others so effective to children as to see their mother taking thoughtful care for those who need it and whom it is in her power to help? What lesson in every moral and religious truth so effective to children as the knowledge that their mother is in all her actions guided by these high precepts?

There can be no doubt that the most effective training for children is the training of example, and this truth the mother needs constantly to bear in mind. How can the impatient, querulous, fault-finding mother teach patience and kindness and good temper? How can the vain mother teach humility? How can the mother greatly absorbed in keeping up with the pomps and vanities of life, eager for place and show, teach her children the true principles of a happy life? How can the selfish mother teach generosity or kindness, or the discontented mother teach contentment?

And right here is one of the fundamental needs of the mother, — the need of being happy in and satisfied with her work in the home. All other ambitions and aims must be subservient to her work there during the period when her children are around her knees or need her constant care. Many a young mother makes here her first mistake. She has been accustomed, perhaps, in her former life to accomplish her own plans and purposes. Perhaps she has been devoted to some specific pursuit to which she gave regular hours and from which she reaped tangible results. Her work in her home and for her children is of such an entirely different nature that it often causes great pain and perplexity. A large part of the actual labor of the home seems to be required for repairing the ravages of daily life, with no progress toward a definite result. Children, with all their beautiful and loving ways, are for the first few years of their lives mainly little animals, and attending to their material needs fills up the mother's time and exhausts her vitality. Keeping them out of mischief absorbs so much of her time that she seems to have little for moral and religious instruction. If the mother allows herself to become discouraged at this period in her home work, to look with longing toward the pursuits and opportunities of women who have no home cares; if she underestimate the honor and value of her work, circumscribed though it appear, — she is in danger of undermining her own comfort and happiness, and consequently the comfort and happiness of the home. She should strengthen her heart by remembering that these confining home duties and cares occupy only a passing period in her life. What if she have not the uninterrupted time she wishes for accomplishing her own plans for study or reading or practice or social intercourse? She is studying the volume of universal human experience. She is learning the joys and sorrows of the

mothers of the human race; she is prac-
tising an art, — incomparably the highest
of all arts, — the moulding of human character; and she must give herself to these
duties with an eye single to their right performance, and with a love for and devotion
to the work which will make her happy in
it. And if the mother thus loves and
honors her work, she will make the atmosphere of the home a happy one under all
ordinary circumstances. Children who
from their earliest recollection remember
their mother as kind and patient and devoted to their best interests, happy in
spending and being spent for them, will
inevitably feel the influence. The many
beautiful instances related of great men
who have risen from the humblest homes,
and of their steadfast devotion to and affection for their faithful though often unlettered mothers, are rich with instruction
and encouragement for all mothers. In
every case such mothers will be found to
have held their children's love by their unselfish devotion to and great love for their
children, and the respect they compelled by

their elevated moral and religious character. How beautiful to hear grown children, who are perhaps far along the road of life themselves, say that, as in early childhood, so in mature years, their mothers are their best, their most valued, consoling, and helpful counsellors!

Poverty and privation strengthen rather than weaken such bonds between mother and children. "We were very, very poor," said a now wealthy business man, talking of his early life; "but it never seemed to us children that we were poor, because our mother always seemed happy with us. She was constantly planning some little pleasure for us that was all our own, and we thought we had the nicest time at home of any children we knew. It was making for us little rabbits or birds out of bread dough, or some molasses candy, or turnover pies in fruit season, or some little thing to give us pleasure and show how she thought of us continually. Then she was always encouraging us to hope for better days, and always hopeful herself for the great things her children were going to do for her when they grew up to be good and useful men. We went to school barefoot and carried with us our dinners, often only corn bread and molasses, but it was always wrapped up in a clean white bit of cloth, so that it might look attractive ; and one of the most touching recollections of my childhood is of seeing my dear mother patiently washing and ironing those bits of white cloth for our school lunches." And when that mother, in after years, was suddenly stricken with a fatal sickness, a special train, chartered with instantaneous haste, took two of those stalwart sons, with all the despatch that money and influence could buy, to that mother's bedside in time to receive her parting words of love and blessing and witness her dying smile.

Such a place, such a kingdom in the hearts of her children, it is worth any mother's toil and care and weariness to win. Outward circumstances need not greatly affect the inner life of the true home or of the faithful, loving mother. Of the home as of the life, it is ever true that " the kingdom of heaven is within." To

such a mother a poet son, after he had
himself nobly encountered and conquered
the severest temptations and trials of life,
addressed these words : —

" Thou type of noblest womanhood!
Thou who in manhood's evil day,
As by the couch of infancy,
　　Still faithful stood;
Unfaltering, and with purpose strong,
Rebuking all the hosts of wrong
With ' Love is more than gift of song,'
　　And ' Virtue is the highest good.'

" Oh, would these wildwood flowers for thee
Were robed in Beauty's charm and bloom,
Made rich with every rare perfume
　　Of poesy;
With every grace of heart and mind,
With woman in all reverence shrined,
In part repaying so in kind
　　A debt as boundless as the sea! "

AN

OLD-FASHIONED ACCOMPLISHMENT.

THE father who said he would rather have his daughter come home from school a fine reader than a fine performer on the piano, if he were compelled to choose between the two accomplishments, was eminently sensible. The mother who said that she would rather have her daughter an accomplished housekeeper than accomplished in all the modern decorative arts, was sensible also. Happily, it is not necessary to choose between these accomplishments, for a capable, healthy young woman may have both ; but it is very necessary to judge wisely as to their relative importance when there is not time and strength for both.

But after all is said and done, — after all the changes wrought in the appearance of our homes by the progress of modern decorative art and by the devices of the modern architect, — what charm is equal to that of a well-kept house? And it is all the more impressive after experience has taught the difficulties to be overcome in modern housekeeping, and given us appreciation of the high order of faculty and administrative ability necessary to carry to perfection the art of living.

The well-kept house can be recognized by its door-step, front door, and hall. Here begins the housekeeper's first battle with her most insidious and persistent annoyer and enemy, dust and dirt. Nothing is more discouraging to the young house-keeper than the fact that things will not stay clean, and no expression is more common than that of wonder where all the dust and soil come from. But it is a fact which must be accepted and to which the housekeeper must adapt herself. The method of the most successful housekeepers seems to be never to let things get out of order or marred with dust and dirt, — to have a regular systematic plan for circumventing the beginnings of evil. When our grandmothers had waxed furniture and bare floors, they waxed and scrubbed every morning regularly, no matter whether the furniture and floors seemed to need it or not. Oh the whiteness of those floors! Oh the polish of that furniture! And so the very noticeably clean look which well-kept houses have, results from systematic and regular " going over " before it is even needed. If the door-plate is polished every morning, it is a small matter to keep it bright; if the steps are washed and the doors wiped every day, they always look fresh; and this is true of every room in the house.

" You must drive housekeeping, or it will drive you," was the motto of one of the most successful of housekeepers, — one who never herself seemed driven by household affairs. Another of her mottoes was, " Eternal vigilance is the price of a clean kitchen," and to the necessity of this vigilance every young housekeeper must make up her mind. As I have said before, for driving housekeeping nothing can equal a good early start in the mornings. The principal exigency that may prevent this will

arise after little children come, when the
mother may have to be awake with them
through the night, in which case, if she
finds herself refreshed by a morning nap,
some arrangement should be made by
which she can take it without hindering
the running of the household machinery.
Forethought and the planning out of the
morning work for others may in a measure overcome this difficulty. As a general
rule, the earlier a house is " cleaned up "
in the morning, the more smoothly will
things run through the day.

The planning and preparation of food is
the next item of importance in good housekeeping, and one where the exercise of
forethought will greatly lessen the care
and monotony of being obliged to get three
meals a day. It is a great convenience to
keep certain kinds of cold meat and meat
jellies, stock for quick soups, and canned
fish and meats, always on hand. It is also
a convenience to have nice dried fruits, jellies, preserves, and marmalades in abundance; and if they are prepared skilfully at
the proper season of the year, they form a

cheap and delightful addition to the larder. A well-arranged storeroom or pantry, with all sorts of groceries carefully and systematically selected and laid in, and replenished before the articles are entirely exhausted, is a necessary department in every well-appointed house. A variety of food is always agreeable and healthful. Many families complain, and with cause, that they get tired of the sameness of the food. It is worth while to give a good deal of thought and attention to securing a variety on the table, and such thought and study will enable a family to have a really large variety of food out of simple materials.

As for the table, the first necessity is abundance of table linen, napkins, etc.; and these should, if possible, be of good quality and always well washed and ironed. There is every difference in the world between the "feel" of a snowy, clean, glossy napkin and one that is poorly washed and ironed. For children a great abundance of bibs is absolutely essential, and for these no material is so suitable as a good quality of towelling, cut off in proper lengths, and then cut to fit the neck of the child. The table-ware may be common delft, but it should be shining clean and bright. Such appointments will make the simplest meal palatable.

Among the many items that a house-keeper has to look closely after, none is more important for the convenience of the household, and none has more annoying results if neglected, than the putting away of clean clothes and the keeping of the clothing of the family generally in proper places. In the training of her family a mother will invariably find the most difficult habit to establish is this of putting things in their proper places. She will for years, in all ordinary cases, have to oversee this department of housekeeping herself, and will have to "keep at" her children about it till their habits are formed. Of course, every child and every member of the family should have his own place, be it ever so small, where he shall keep his own things. To keep things in their places is almost one half the work of housekeeping. Scarcely anything is more discouraging to

the mother than the difficulty so often experienced in forming habits of order in
this direction. One thing, however, may
safely be asserted, that it is of no use to
scold about it. Children should be required to pick up and put away their own
things, and each should be held personally
responsible for his own things or for the
disorder he creates. In many households
there is often a great deal of general scolding and complaining that " somebody " has
put things out of order or left things out
of place, the only effect of which is to
create a pervasively disagreeable and uncomfortable atmosphere without accomplishing any good. The guilty escape in
the general distribution of blame and reproof, and the innocent feel the injustice
of being included in the general category.
In all cases, if possible, find and call to
account the guilty individual. It is a plan
that has been found to work well by many
mothers, to call the heedless ones from
their play or lessons in order to require
them to put their books or clothes or
rooms in order. A child who knows by

experience that if he leaves his boots or his soiled collar or coat in the wrong place he stands a chance of being sent for at school or when he is in the midst of a game and being kindly but firmly compelled to put his things in order, will probably, in course of time, learn to think of such things beforehand.

As for the thousand and one things about a house which get out of order and for which nobody seems responsible, the mother must take the care and responsibility of them patiently upon her own shoulders, especially while her children are small, and, either with her own hands or by special directions to servants, must keep things in order. Here, too, the chief secret seems to be not to let things get out of order. The art of picking up things, of putting them away before they accumulate in disorder, is most necessary to successful housekeeping. To be sure, it is often a thankless, wearying task; it seems to consume day after day with no appreciable progress; it is like constant pumping simply to keep water from rising instead of a labor to fill something; it is negative; it is work that attracts attention only when it is not done; but it is nevertheless one of the things most absolutely essential to the comfort of a home. The mother is the special providence of the house in small things as well as great, and in the home nothing is small that results in comfort or discomfort, ill temper or amiability. In the long performance of this task upon which every wife enters when she assumes the responsibilities of wifehood, she has need of those two fundamental household virtues, — untiring patience and a deep-seated sense of duty.

A USEFUL HOUSEHOLD MAXIM.

AN Oriental sage was once asked by his sovereign, also a wise and good man, to give him a saying that should be appropriate and restraining in times of prosperity and happiness, and also a consolation and comfort in times of adversity and sorrow. Difficult as was the task of finding some sentiment or truth that would be consonant with these widely opposite conditions, even the wise ruler was satisfied when the sage gave him the saying, " Even this shall pass away;" and it is said that he had it engraved upon a ring which he wore ever after.

But whether the ruler of a great empire found this a useful maxim or not, certain it is, that for the ruler of the smaller empire of the home, the mother, it is a very comforting little sentence, and, if reflected upon, may oftentimes help her in those difficulties and trials in household life which

can only be overcome by patience. The
thread of family life, even in the best-regulated homes, has an inherent tendency
to get into snarls. As Mrs. Stowe says:
" There never yet was that home or family
where everything could be made to run 'just
so.' " Things are always happening in the
most unexpected manner; the best and most
systematic plans are inadequate to meet all
the emergencies that arise when the different individualities of parents, children, and
servants all act and react upon one another.
The best plan by which these roughnesses,
these tangles, can be straightened out, is to
wait a little, to let time help overcome the
difficulty; and in order to do this cheerfully,
it is well to say to ourselves, " Even this
shall pass away."

Take, for instance, the discomfort and
confusion that may overtake an ordinary-
sized family when, on awaking some early
autumn morning, a cold, foggy, dismal, un-
seasonable rain is found to be falling. A
fire must be built in the sitting-room or
nursery on account of the baby or the very
little ones, and the chimney will be almost

4

sure to smoke. Warm garments are needed
and called for by all the members of the
family, and must be hunted out from among
the packed-away winter clothing, which
probably only the mother knows where or
how to find, if indeed she does, in the
sudden call for them. But the baby cries
and demands her whole attention. The
discomfort of the morning affects the spirit
and temper of the cook as well as the
kitchen fire. As is the way with all uncultivated spirits, she makes it an excuse for
grumbling, bad service, and in nine cases
out of ten for positive insubordination and
impertinence. The boys and men about the
house are unreasonable and impatient in
their demands for service and attention,
and altogether it is a very uncomfortable
domestic atmosphere that pervades the
house. How easy under such circumstances
for the house-mother to give way to temper,
and give utterance to harsh words that shall
add tenfold to the general discomfort, and
to say sharp and cutting things that shall
leave the sting of unhappiness for days and
weeks to come! How easy for her, also,

to make her own labors more difficult and complicated by allowing the conduct of her servants to irritate her into discharging them on the spot, or doing or saying some other rash thing which, while it affords·a momentary gratification to temper or a sense of power, reacts with most damaging and mortifying results upon her own convenience and comfort! How much better for her to reflect that in a little time these annoyances and this condition of things must necessarily pass away, and to preserve good temper and speak in gentle tones amid the surrounding confusion! And if the mother will but control her spirit and take a few moments for reflection, if she will but look up and beyond, even in the midst of labors, inconveniences, and discomforts, to what heights of spiritual serenity and comfort may she not attain! And thus lifted above the earthly and material plane of life, she may calmly view and firmly guide the course of the domestic storm, and shortly diffuse over all the sunshine and calm of her own cheerful, unperturbed spirit.

And so of scores and hundreds of emergencies that happen, and that will happen, to every house-mother. The sudden or lingering sickness of her children may throw all household methods into disorder; the necessity for changing servants on account of incapacity or insubordination will for a time disturb and roughen the whole current of family life ; the unexpected visitors, the inopportune callers, at times will discommode her and interfere with her plans of work; the muddy day comes, and the children spoil their clothes and track mud all over the house; the seamstress fails to come at the appointed time, or spoils the garments which are needed in haste ; financial circumstances compel the use of outworn or inconvenient articles of furniture and clothing, or the doing without needed articles altogether. All these things distract and annoy and trouble; but they are only aggravated by being met in a complaining, irritable spirit. Far, far better to possess one's soul in patience and say, " Even this shall pass away."

But a far deeper import will attach in the faithful mother's mind to this helpful

and instructive saying when it is applied
to the imperative, all-absorbing, and often
exhausting care of little children. The
mother's life is frequently so wholly filled
with providing for the material wants of her
children, that its springs seem for the time
being to become dried up and to lose all
freshness and beauty. She has no leisure
for reading, for the practice of her accomplishments, for intercourse with friends, or
for any of the recreations of life. Patience,
tired mother! These children are growing
up; they will not always be little and fretful and troublesome; the house will not
always be noisy and always getting out of
order. Those boys will soon be in school,
then in college, then gone from home to
trouble or brighten it no more. The little
girls that make so many demands on you
for aprons and buttons and doll dresses,
will soon be grown to womanhood, and
then gone to homes of their own. Then
you can have order in your house; then
you can have leisure and quiet. Be as
happy as you can, even in these busy, care-
crowded days. Think how dreadful it

would be to miss one troublesome little
noise-maker from among the flock.

> " The mother in the sunshine sits
>   Beside the cottage wall;
> And softly while she knits and knits
>   The gathering tears down fall:
> The little hindering thing is gone,
> And undisturbed she may knit on."

In one other very important period in
her children's lives will the thoughtful
mother find the deepest import to this little saying. Nearly all children, especially
nearly all boys, pass through a period in
the development of their characters when
they seem wilful, unconscientious, impatient
of reproof, sour, and rude. It is a period
requiring the greatest patience and wisdom
on the part of parents ; and children must
be led, and cannot be driven, through it.
It is in some degree the result of the mental and moral as well as physical struggles
that are a part of the development from
childhood to manhood or womanhood. Love
and gentleness only can restrain now ; for
the boy and the girl are passing into the
period when, if restrained at all, they must

restrain themselves. But by the grace of God even this period will pass away; and faithful parents are often permitted to receive out of it sons and daughters who are spiritually new creatures; and so the maxim of the ancient sage and the words of the Apostle teach the same lesson: " Even this shall pass away," and " Ye have need of patience, that after ye have done the will of God ye may receive the promise."

THE RELATIVE IMPORTANCE OF THINGS.

"IF we only had a few less curtains and a few more comforts!" was the half-jocose, half-earnest complaint of a young husband who had intrusted to a young wife the modest sum he had laid aside for furnishing a house, and which she had expended for that purpose. She had a taste for beautiful things, and their home was indeed charming to look upon; but the working experience of every-day life had soon shown many essentials of comfort to be sadly lacking. There was a dearth of conveniences for the kitchen; a dearth of good sensible every-day towelling and bed linen and blankets. There were one or two very fine table-cloths with napkins to match, intended to be used only on special occasions, while there were not enough of the plainer kinds to keep the every-day table fresh and attractive. There were lace curtains all over the house, but not enough bed comforts to furnish the beds for winter. There was a beautiful set of decorated china for company use, but a marked deficiency in the number and quality of dishes suitable and intended for every-day use. The young wife, at that stage of her experience, had not learned the relative importance of things.

" Why not use the decorated china and fine table-cloths every day?" queries some prospective young housekeeper who has a high and beautiful ideal of what the home table should be, and who has not yet learned by experience what it costs in vitality and energy to maintain this ideal. This also is merely a question of the relative importance of things. If the housekeeper be so situated that she can command time to take care of her china herself, or such competent service as will secure its being well taken care of by others, so that her mind and temper will not be in a constant strain and vexation about it, the decorated china for every-day use is all right and very enjoyable. But in the large majority of homes, especially after little children come, the every-day care of fine china is a temptation and a snare. It is pitiable to think of the amount of real mental suffering endured by many a young mother and housekeeper over the spoliation of her beautiful table furniture by the careless, unskilled handling of ordinary household help. There is, however, so much real suffering to be endured in life that cannot possibly be avoided that it is surely the part of wisdom to abate, so far as lies in one's power, every abatable cause of pain and annoyance. Peace of mind, relief from petty care, freedom from irritating circumstances, are of far more importance to the young wife and mother than all the decorated china in the world. Put it away, weary housekeeper and mother, — what is left of it, — in the china-closet; get a good substantial set of white stoneware that will only need to be kept well washed to make your table inviting, and which it will not break your heart to have broken. You will be surprised and delighted to find what a relief you will experience, and with what equanimity you can

henceforth hear the ominous clatterings
and crashes from the kitchen sink. Do
this while your children are small. When
your baby girls grow up to be young women,
let them get out and use and take care of
the decorated china if they choose. You
can enjoy it then without the present draw-
backs. You need your time, strength, patience, and vitality for other things just
now.

To reduce the amount of care and the
friction of the machinery of home life is the
one constant problem of the housekeeper
and homekeeper. It is the sphinx riddle
propounded to every young mother. The
sphinx destroyed all who could not solve
her riddles. So, too, the young mother
who cannot solve the riddle of the relative
importance of the innumerable demands
upon her time and attention is in danger of
being destroyed mentally and physically.
Everything cannot be done; everything
cannot be cared for. It requires discretion
and common sense of such a high order
that it may well be called wisdom, to
proportion rightly one's time and care

among the unending, perplexing demands
of home life. One thing, however, is certain : the higher should never be sacrificed
to the lower. If it is a question between an
elaborate meal, with a wearied, overtaxed,
nervous woman presiding over it, or a simple meal, with a fresh, unworn, cheerful
mistress behind the tea-tray, who would hesitate as to the answer? If it is a question
between a few elaborate dresses and embroidered petticoats for the new baby, or a
great abundance of little slips and pinning
blankets, simple, cheap, and easily laun-
dered, what sensible young mother ought
to hesitate ? If it is a question between taking excellent and constant care of two or
three little ones and the proper care of a
great window full of house-plants, by all
means let the house-plants go, or save only
one or two whose care will not materially
increase the aggregate amount of care.

A constant and wise discretion must be
exercised by the house-mother in deciding
as to the relative importance of the different
kinds of work to be done in the home. The
great danger of American young mothers is

nerves; and physicians tell us that disordered nerves are the result of overwork and anxiety, or of too great mental tension in one direction. It is not well for a mother to have the too unceasing care of her children; change and relaxation are needed even from this labor of love. The mothers who suffer most from weariness in the care of children are those who board, and who are therefore constantly confined with their children. Mother and children act and react upon one another, physically and mentally, till both are nervous and impatient simply for lack of change of surroundings and an occasional new atmosphere. Any observer of children knows that the least troublesome children are those where the mother, dividing her care for them with other household cares, often leaves them to themselves to seek their own amusement. But while doing this the mother must not overtax her strength in other work. She must remember that it is of the first importance that she keep herself in good physical condition. No temptation to "overdo" in the direction of entertaining company, giving elaborate teas or dinners, or even canning and preserving fruit or getting the spring or fall sewing done, should be allowed to overcome her judgment as to the relative importance of such work. Her first duty is, as far as possible, to be a cheerful, healthy, happy, patient, and loving mother; and all work that tends to prevent her from fulfilling this duty is comparatively unimportant and would better be left undone.

A FEW years ago a little poem was printed in a somewhat obscure newspaper, which at once began to be copied far and wide. Evidently it had touched some common heart-experience, and thus won immediate and wide-spread recognition; yet it was the narration in verse of a very simple little story. The opening verses represented the farmer's wife wearily contemplating the toils and cares of the day that lay before her, and the refrain of each verse was, —

" 'T is a wonder girls will wed."

But evening came, and with it the farmer, who, as he prepares for supper, praises his wife's neat kitchen and the savory meal she has in readiness for him, and then says that no other farmer in all the country round has such a smart, good wife as he, and that all the neighbors know it and envy him his happy home. All of which so changes the feelings of the farmer's wife that she forgets her complaints and weariness in rejoicing that she has such a good, kind husband, and the conclusion she finally expresses is, —

    " 'T is no wonder girls will wed."

All of which conveys simply and beautifully the lesson that there is no sweetener of daily toil like a loving appreciativeness. It is a grace of the spirit that is especially valuable and uplifting in the home, and that should be carefully cultivated and frequently permitted expression. Every one knows by experience the effect, even upon the physical strength, of words of appreciation and encouragement. The story is familiar of the fireman who was attempting to scale a perilous ladder in order to save a human life jeopardized in a burning building. He seemed to waver and be almost ready to abandon his attempt, when some one in the crowd below cried, " Cheer him ! " The crowd caught at the suggestion and sent up cheer after cheer, which so reinvigorated the almost exhausted man that he redoubled his efforts and energy, and the jeopardized life was saved. There is scarcely any human being who is not susceptible to the effect of words of encouragement and appreciation. Few advance so far in any path of success that they are beyond caring for such words, and scarcely any are so callous through ignorance or oppression that they cannot be inspired to effort by words of kindness and encouragement.

But it is in the home especially that the grace of appreciativeness is most valuable and beautiful. Much of the work pertaining to home life is monotonous and wearing, and this is true of the work of both wife and husband. Unless loving appreciation sweetens and elevates daily toil, married life is in great danger of degenerating into a humdrum, prosaic, depressing routine of care and work. The husband is apt to make everything subservient to his getting to business in the morning, and in the evening he comes home with exhausted vitality and wishes only for an opportunity to rest. But if he have an appreciative heart, full of love for the wife who has all day " tarried with the stuff," he can easily brighten all the atmosphere of the home by a few words that will show that he can forget himself to think of her and her cares and toils. He can let her know how glad he is to reach the haven of home after the day's turmoil ; he can take notice of the pleasant orderly house and the well-appointed table, and give his wife credit for these good results of her labor.   Or if she has been prevented from accomplishing all that might be desirable in these respects, he can lighten her anxiety and comfort her heart by refraining from fault-finding, and by words of palliation for whatever may be unaccomplished.   " Better is a dinner of herbs where love is than a stalled ox and hatred therewith," said the inspired writer ; and no fact of home or married life is more apparent than that loving appreciation and sympathy will lighten and alleviate all domestic trials and difficulties, and heighten all domestic joys.

Corresponsively, the same kind of considerate appreciativeness is due from the

wife to the husband. Men are not so dependent as women on the strength that
comes from the love and cheer of home,
because they have the constant stimulus
of outward circumstance, and the ambitions
and competitions of business to inspire
them. Yet few men are incapable of being
cheered and better fitted to meet the daily
anxieties and confining toil which business
life imposes, by words of loving appreciation from wife and children. Conjugal love
is doubtless a hardy plant; but too often
its root, strong and vital though it be, is
kept buried out of sight, while the blossoms
and beauty it might develop in a right sunshine and atmosphere are almost wholly
missed out of the home.

But there is a twofold truth in regard
to appreciation and sympathy and their
expression, that needs to be carefully recognized: they must not be too constantly
drawn upon, and they must meet with quick
and loving response. The fountain of human sympathy has a tendency to stop flow-
ing when drawn upon too imperiously or
too frequently. Words of appreciation and

love will soon cease when they are listened to with a chill and forbidding air. Many a husband, returning from his own day's toil and finding his wife burdened and weary with the care of house and family, would be glad to speak words of cheer and sympathy, but they go unsaid because his wife is " in a temper." She has already such a high appreciation of these trials that his mention of them tends only to exaggerate her own estimate of them, and deepen her sense of being a much abused and imposed upon woman. If there is any one mental attitude or disposition that will instantly check the expression of sympathy and appreciation, it is this. If persisted in, it will as surely dry up both the fountains and the streams of household affection as the winter's cold will turn to ice the mountain spring and running brook.

SCOLDING.

NO woman who would retain her true ascendency in her family can afford to scold. It is the most undignified, belittling, disenchanting, self-disrespecting performance that any one can engage in at any time or under any circumstances; but it is especially so in the case of a mother and housekeeper.

Scolding may be distinguished from the giving of reproof, for which there is often occasion in the best-regulated families, by its being an expression of personal irritability, and by the intended effect of producing irritation and discomfort in those around. Its most frequent form of expression is a sort of generalization which is usually false, from some single difficulty which is irremediable except by specific action. "You children are the most disorderly creatures I have ever seen; you leave your hats in one place and your books

in another, and keep me forever picking up
after you," says the petulant mother. " If
you don't pick up your things better I
will — " and here follow the ineffectual
threats of the scolding mood. The words
are worse than thrown away ; they do positive harm. The child who is at fault on
the occasion escapes conviction through
the general accusation and blame thrown
upon all, while the children who are not at
fault are irritated and resent the injustice.
A moment's reflection would convince a
sensible mother that such petulant, useless
complaint would accomplish no good ; but
this is really not her object. She feels
uncomfortable, discommoded, and irritated,
and disposed to vent her irritation on those
around, and to make them sharers in her
discomfort. The true way to remedy disorder among children is kindly but firmly
to compel each one to pick up and put
away and take care of his own things. To
accomplish this may often require severe
reproof and even punishment, but it should
be administered individually, and if possible privately, with tone and manner free

from personal irritation, and with especial care not to lay the blame for the disorder on those who are not responsible for it.

So of the scores and hundreds of occasions in family life which try the temper of the mistress. If the cook is careless and sends the meals to the table improperly prepared, how useless, how disagreeable, for the mistress of the house to utter a general tirade against cooks during the progress of the meal! How worse than useless afterward for her to tell the cook that as a class cooks are worthless, wasteful, and incompetent, that they don't earn their wages, and to indulge in harsh epithets and threats! There is no quicker way to lose the respect of servants and to demoralize them than to scold at them in a general way when irritated. All faults charged should be specifically named, and the requirement made positive that such faults must be remedied. This is the only way consistent with the dignity of a mistress, and it is too often rendered nugatory by the fact that mistresses are not in a position to present an alternative. They are more dependent upon servants, in our present condition of household service, than servants are upon them. But at all events scolding only makes matters worse, not better.

Scolding is, in fact, either the weak expedient of a character too weak to remedy or remove evils, or it is the weapon and defence of the inferior.

> " For every evil under the sun
>   There is a remedy or there 's none :
>   If there is a remedy, find it ;
>   If there is not, never mind it."

Here is a husband who has certain habits which irritate and discommode his wife. She revenges herself by scolding, and by declaring that he always does such things ; that all men are naturally selfish and mean, and more words to the same effect, which cause irritation only. Nothing could be more derogatory to a wife's influence than such a course. She should decide to force an issue by firmness and determination, and compel a respect for her rights and wishes in family matters, or she should make up her mind to overlook such pecu-

liarities and arrange her life accordingly.
Either she must cure the evil or adapt herself to it; but let her not on any account
degrade herself to scold about it.

But if a scolding woman is so disgraceful
and discordant a factor in a family, what
shall be said of a scolding man? The man
who, because business has gone wrong, or
customers have deceived him, or employees
have cheated him, comes home and vents
his irritability on his family, is wholly inex-
cusable. It is amusing to notice how a
scolding man often displays, in an exaggerated form, the very weaknesses and
follies that are usually charged more particularly upon women. He, too, will gener-
alize from one fact in a most inconsequent
way. If the room is too warm, he will declare that it is always like an oven; if it is
too cold, he will assert that his wife never
has enough fuel put in the fire; if the table
is not up to the standard, he will wonder
why he can never get a decent meal at
home; if the children are fretful, they are
the crossest, worse-trained children ever
known; if the servants make a mistake,

the whole race of servants is denounced, and the denunciation is usually wound up with the declaration that women are not fit to manage servants anyway, and that their insubordination and failures are all owing to women's incompetency to train and govern them. A man, by a single evening's scolding, can disseminate enough discomfort and irritability through a household to make everybody uncomfortable for a week.

Everywhere and under all circumstances, scolding has this distinguishing characteristic: it is intended to wound somebody, to hurt somebody, to make somebody uncomfortable, not with a remedial design, but simply as a relief to an inward personal irritation. Its effect on family life is like throwing sand into a delicate machine; it causes all parts to grate upon each other; it does no good, but only evil, and that continually.

TOO INDUSTRIOUS.

NO observer of the common methods of household life, especially among that large class who are in medium circumstances, neither poor nor rich, but in the main comfortable, can fail to be struck with the different way in which men and women regard and use leisure time. In fact, it is a question whether the majority of the mistresses of such homes ever know what it is to enjoy a bit of genuine leisure. They are always oppressed with a sense of the necessity of chipping some odd bit of work into every chink of leisure time. This is industry pushed to the point where it becomes a vice, and often makes a very disagreeable element in domestic life.

For instance, a member of the family wishes to read aloud some interesting article or poem. The busy mother listens with apparent interest and enjoyment, but the work in her hands is, after all, of paramount importance, and she does not hesitate to interrupt the reader at the most interesting part of the narrative with the request to "Stop till I try on this apron I am making Willie," or "Wait a moment while I go downstairs and press out this seam;" or if the work is not actually in her hands, her mind is running on houschold cares, and with a kind of double consciousness that occasionally breaks out in such exclamations as "Stop a little till I call to the cook to set batter cakes for breakfast," or "I wonder if Bridget has put the clothes to soak for the washing to-morrow," all of which remarks have the most chilling and even exasperating effect upon the interested reader and listeners, who justly regard such interruptions as trivial and unworthy. We all remember how Jean Paul Richter, in his "Flower, Fruit, and Thorn Pieces," paints the attempts of the good Advocate of the Poor, Firmian Stanislaus, to interest and instruct his pretty but commonplace little wife, and to elevate her mentally by reading to her his productions, and of the delight that filled his heart when one

evening he seemed to have secured her most
earnest attention. The knitting in her
hands fell to her lap, and her eyes were
fixed intently on the floor. He was just
completing one of his finest periods, and
noticing her rapt air he exclaimed to himself, "She understands, she appreciates!"
When he ceased she looked at him earnestly and said, "Don't forget to leave off
that left stocking in the morning; I must
darn that hole in the toe." It was the poor
advocate's last attempt to secure his wife's
interest and attention for his poems. From
that time their paths diverged till death.

The same abnormally developed habit of
industry appears more frequently to the
extreme detriment of women whose health
is feeble through over-work or care of children. The weary mother has been laid up
with a headache. What she needs afterward is absolute rest and recreation. As
soon as she can sit up on the sofa, instead
of calling for an interesting book or maga-
zine and seeking pure diversion, she says,
" Hand me that basket of stockings, I think
I can darn a few of them;" or " Bring me

Johnny's trousers, I will put a patch in the knee." And if unable to do these things, she lets her mind get in a fret and fever because her work is getting so behindhand, which is even worse than to attempt to perform the work herself.

Fancy how it would seem to have men act so around the house! Imagine a man recovering from a headache, asking for the hatchet and a piece of pine board, and saying he " might just as well be splitting up a lot of kindlings," or that as he does n't feel very well he " will try to mend that broken chair." Men recover from a slight indisposition sooner and more thoroughly than women simply because they make a business of getting well, just as they do of everything else.

Women have been so long preached to about the necessity of being industrious and of improving their time, and they are withal so burdened with the thousand details of unorganized work, which makes all household labor seem to accomplish so little, that they need rather to consider now how to withdraw their minds and hands from constant household occupation, and learn to rest and refresh themselves so as to have an interest in the world outside of home. What is the reason so many faithful mothers lose their hold on their children when they attain to manhood and womanhood to so much greater extent than the father, who is equally busy in his store? It is because the too industrious mother has failed to keep abreast of the current of thought and information, and has lost interest in the general movements around her. She thought she could not spare time to read or to mingle in society. Her very devotion to her children and her home has dwarfed her nature. She is never easy except when she is at work. One of the most painful aspects, often, of such a mistaken course of conduct is the utter inability of those most interested to arrest it. How often do husband and father plead, "Oh, mother, do put that work away; do rest yourself!" and how often does such a request seem only to inspire a determination to do more, while the chagrin and impatience with which such misguided industry is regarded by other members of the family is set down to lack of appreciation or to an unkind spirit. Industry is an excellent thing in woman, as well as in man; but there is a possibility of its being practised to a degree that changes it from a virtue to a vice. To choose the happy medium and golden mean should be the study of every sensible young wife and mother.

"WHAT more can I give my children than I am giving them?" asked an anxious young mother of a matron who had successfully reared a large family. "I think, my dear, they would be benefited by a little wholesome neglect," was the reply. It was the result of keen observation, and a recognition of the fact that the children in question were kept in a continual state of worry by being constantly watched, — the mother's vigilance being so incessant that their spontaneity was checked, and, as one remarked, life for them was one eternal "Don't!"

Said another, in relating reminiscences of childhood: "When I was a child I was rendered miserable by being constantly watched and trained. I was very fond of being alone at times. I could give no reason for it, but I loved to stay in unoccupied rooms, or find a hiding-place among the bushes in the garden, there to amuse myself

with my own plays and fancies. My mother
was suspicious that this meant evil of some
kind; and constant surveillance and repri-
mand for going off by myself are among the
unpleasant memories of my childhood."

Nothing should be more carefully respected and guarded than the individuality
of a child. The atmosphere of home should
be that of love and safety, in which all the
natural inclinations of children should be
allowed to act spontaneously. Their wishes
for employments and possessions of their
own should be respected, their tastes in
matters of food and dress consulted in so
far as is consistent with the convenience of
those around. We have heard grown-up
people tell of the distaste they had when
children for certain kinds of food which they
were compelled to eat, or certain kinds of
clothes which they were compelled to wear.
It used to be a rule in many families brought
up in the Puritan style that a child must eat
all the crusts of his bread, or all the fat on
his meat, or all the food on his plate. Such
rules are barbarous, and we trust nearly
obsolete; yet children's taste in food ought

to be more considered than it is. Food
that is distasteful should never be forced
upon them; and to procure for them food
which they enjoy, will in most cases be to
procure such food as their systems require.
So of taste in dress. Children will sometimes have an antipathy to particular colors
or particular garments, and a preference
for others. If possible, these tastes should
always be respected, guarding, of course,
against encouraging or fostering vanity.

So of the occupations and employments
of children : as far as possible they should
be left to follow their own inclinations
when they are harmless. If your little girl
would rather play with hammer and tacks
than with dolls, why, let her have them,
and see that she has a board or a place
where she can drive them without reproof.
If your little boy always wants to hitch the
chairs up for horses, and can enjoy himself
happily as an imaginary stage-driver, why,
set apart certain chairs for him, and let him
drive unmolested and unwatched. If he
begs for tools, let him have them; if he
wants pencils or paints, procure them for

him. The only way by which parents can secure the confidence of their children is first to show confidence in them. Confidence must be won ; it can never be forced, not even from the little ones who play around our knees.

A happy childhood is the greatest heritage parents can give to their children. Its memory will brighten and cheer the whole of life. To be happy it must to a certain extent be unrestrained. The home playground should have no dangerous places needing to be guarded, and where children must be forbidden. And in the shelter of the home and the playground let the young spirits develop freely, spontaneously, happily. Let them have their little secrets, their own possessions which no one shall interfere with, their own plays, and, so far as is consistent with the welfare and comfort of others, their own way. Life will discipline them harshly enough when parents can no longer shield them from sorrow. Happy the home to which the child can look back and say, as does a beloved English author, —

" Well, I have been happy once! I have been a child! I have been in heaven! I have stood in the smile and lain in the arms of one of God's angels. I was the happy child of a gentle, loving mother.

" Oh that garden of my early home, where I and the flowers grew up together! I and Time were playfellows then; I feared him not. I once saw a picture which had for its subject an hour-glass standing on a pedestal, and a child looking calmly and steadfastly at it. In vain — so I interpreted the picture — in vain the sands were falling fast and unremittingly; the child looked calmly on. What did it care for time? It was not afraid of all its past, or all its coming hours, still less that the hours should cease to flow for it. In one sense the child is living in eternity. With all its microscopic vision it has no bounds to its future. Insect-like, it beats its little wing in the quite limitless air.

" But the light of that garden, and the light of all the world to me, was my mother's love, my mother's smile."

HOME COMFORT.

THE most pleasant impression that any house or home can give, or that any individual can give, is that of being suffused with, or diffusing a sense of, comfort. There are homes which give an impression of comfort immediately when one enters the door. There are people who, without any particular charm, are charming because they impress us with a feeling that they are comfortable people to live with. There are homes of abundant means where there is an entire absence of an air of comfort or repose. A distinguished man who was for a time a frequent visitor at the home of another complained of its lack of quiet and comfort, because, as he said, the good lady of the house always seemed to be scrubbing or cleaning something. She was never in a condition of repose and comfort herself, and hence made a most uncomfortable impression on all who saw her in her home.

Fortunately for the great majority of home-makers, comfort depends but little on the possession of large means. In fact, the homes of the rich are not in the general average remarkable for an appearance of home comfort. Great parlors, with costly furniture and curtains and upholstery that one almost fears to use, deserted for the most part by the family, chilly and forbidding, are the most striking features of many a costly mansion. The visitor in such a home will generally find the real comfort-centre of the house to be some room with plain furniture and carpets, devoted perhaps to the children or to some department of household work. On the other hand the real comfort-maker, with a minimum of things to work with, can invest an almost bare room with the appearance and reality of comfort. Given a good stove, a few rugs or a plain carpet, and a very poor room may be made comfortable. Paper or cotton will shut the wintry wind from its entrance between the window sashes; a few boards and nails and some bright-colored chintz will be sufficient material out of which to evoke the comfortable lounge ; the same inexpensive material will cushion the easy-chair ; a very cheap table is as good as mahogany or marble if it has a cover on it ; a brightly burning lamp with a clean, bright chimney throws the best gas in the shade ; and with these cheap materials any person with the gift of making things comfortable can have an attractive and comfortable room.

The comfort-dispenser in a home usually is a woman. Sometimes it is a man. There are not a few men in the world who have a genius for helping to make things comfortable around home. They are the ones who keep an eye to little things that break or go wrong or get misplaced about a house, and who are not above remedying such difficulties at once. The swollen door that will not shut, or the broken pane of glass, or the door-knob that has worked off, or the storm-door that needs to be put on or taken off, or the pump that needs a new handle or a new valve, — none of these things are beneath their notice and attention. They are the ones who keep an eye

on the wood-pile and the coal-bin, and above
all on the kindling, and feel a sense of responsibility in having these things provided. Happy the wife whose husband, if
need be, takes care that she is provided with
kindling! Such a man is almost sure to
be a model husband and a true comfort-
dispenser. One of the most touching and
characteristic incidents in the life of Lydia
Maria Child is her home-coming after her
husband's funeral. They had been a de-
votedly attached and remarkably happy
couple. She had striven to bear up under
the blow of his loss, and had to some degree
been able to do so. But on returning to
her widowed home, her eye caught sight of
the many little things done by her husband
that showed how he planned for her comfort. He had banked up the foundation of
their little cottage; he had covered her
flower-beds with straw and filled the little
outside kitchen with wood and kindling
ready to her hand. And the sight of all
these thoughtful provisions for her comfort overwhelmed her with a sense of love
and loss.

Comfort and repose go together. No person is comfortable to live with who is always " on the go," always planning or executing some work, like the poor lady who was always scrubbing something. The work of the comfortable person is done " without observation." But little is said about it. As with good manners, unobtrusiveness is one of the prime elements in comfort. " Nothing in excess" is one of its fundamental rules. Truly it is one of the best and most laudable ambitions of life to surround one's self with, and to be a source of, genuine comfort.

LIVING TOGETHER.

IT is questioned by many whether advance in civilization and culture really increases the sum total of human happiness or not. Our faculties are cultivated so that we see and feel and enjoy much of beauty in form and color and agreeableness in manners that is unappreciated in ruder stages of life and progress; but as a necessary result we become more keenly sensitive to ugliness, inharmony, and boorish manners. The cultivated musical ear takes intense delight in Beethoven, Mozart, and Haydn, but is correspondingly tortured by the wheezing hand-organ that delights the street boys. The cultivated taste in dress revels in the beauty of graceful drapery and harmonious combinations of color and material; but as a penalty, its possessor is made miserable by an ill-fitting glove or boot, or by being compelled to wear coarse garments.

A corresponding change takes place in the social feelings as we become sensible, through culture, of all the subtle influences that human beings exert upon one another by conduct or manners. In the earlier and ruder stages of society whole families of the early pioneers were, many of them, reared in one or two rooms; and right happy did they seem to be in their rough-and-tumble jostling life, where there was no privacy, no opportunity for being alone, and all had all things pretty much in common. Now, society has so far changed that their children all want homes where every member can have his own private room; and to be compelled to be too closely associated personally causes serious discomfort. It is the penalty of culture.

So, too, in the family relationship and the different modes of expressing affection or displeasure, of inflicting pain or inspiring delight. The rude boor who strikes his wife a heavy blow or swears at her in a moment of temporary anger, does not begin to inflict the exquisite pain that the cultivated gentleman can inflict upon his gentle wife by the expression of the countenance or the tone of a cutting word. A poor Irishwoman was once engaged in scrubbing the front steps of a marble mansion, when the master came home from a journey. " Oh," she said to the mistress, " how happy ye ought to be that yer husband comes home to you, and is not drunk or abusin' you, or beatin' the childer, like my old man does sometimes." And yet the poor Irishwoman was the happier wife of the two.

It is often remarked, and probably truthfully, that parents are much gentler and more considerate with their children than parents used to be. Certain it is, there is far less corporal punishment and far more indulgence of children than formerly. But now we begin to perceive that there may even be a tyranny of love. We see that people can even suffer exquisitely from being overburdened by a love that fetters and prevents the free expansion of the faculties. The nearest and dearest of relatives, parents and children, brothers and sisters, can inflict pain upon each other by a selfish affection, that is satisfied with nothing short of absorbing the life of the beloved object; that insists on constant companionship when that companionship and surveillance may be exhausting in the most painful degree.

One of the things most essential for preserving happiness in a high state of culture, is the respecting of the individuality of each one. That is the highest and best style of home where there is the least friction between differing individualities, and this is the best secured by allowing each one the fullest possible liberty that is consistent with the rights of all. There are families where one member cannot have a particular friend, or a little secret plan of his own, without exciting the suspicion and jealousy of the rest; or where one member of the family cannot be invited out without offending the other members of the family: where, if one member of the family fancies a particular style of dress or kind of amusement or mode of employment, the rest seem to feel warranted in making irritating criticisms and remarks. Again, there are families where the ill temper of one will be permitted to darken the whole atmosphere of the home, and render every one uncomfortable.

"You cannot tell much about a family until you have both summered and wintered with them," said a lady who had seen much of life. Few, perhaps, are the families where one who summers and winters with them does not find some great inharmony at some time or other. This ought not so to be. No husband and wife are fit to create a home who are not able by self-control, by forbearance, by gentleness, by restraint of hasty speech, by a cultivation of the sense of justice, by generosity, by appreciation of their own and their children's diverse needs and natures, to make an atmosphere of perpetual summer which shall also be an atmosphere of freedom; where no unreasonable storms of temper ever break, and no unnecessary restraint is imposed upon the free expression of the individuality of all members of the family. Only such a home is worthy the name in this stage of the progress and civilization of the nineteenth century.

THE DOMESTIC SERVICE PROBLEM.

A VERY intelligent and highly cultivated woman, who for years had
taught advanced classes in a fine private
school, was married somewhat late in life.
On the eve of her marriage, and while preparing the outfit for her new home, she
was heard to remark: "On one point I
am resolved: when I am married and have
a home of my own, I never will allow myself to fall into the habit of making the
difficulties I may have with my servants,
and their shortcomings, a topic of conversation, as do the majority of the married
ladies I meet."

Ten years afterward the same lady, now
the mother of four beautiful children, meeting the same friends, said: "I no longer
wonder that the servant question is the
chief topic of conversation among women.
Why, it is the bane of domestic life! The

difficulty of managing household help is the ever deepening cloud which destroys home comfort, disarranges every plan, makes a housekeeper's life a burden, and spreads disorder in every nook and corner of the house. Until this problem is solved it is in vain for women to plan for home comfort, for self-improvement, for methods of training for their children, or anything else that requires leisure and freedom from annoying care."

Perhaps there is no more discouraging feature in this vexed question than the slighting and even contemptuous opinion with which many men regard it; for not until their earnest co-operation is secured can the problem ever be solved. Men are sensitive enough to the annoyances arising from bad domestic service. They are quick enough to remark upon badly cooked food, untidy kitchens and back-yards, wastefulness in fuel and provisions, unskilful laundry-work on their linen, and the thousand and one failures on the part of servants; yet he is a rare man who does not, in the main, set these failures down to the supposed fact that his wife does not know how to manage servants, that women cannot control help, and in all probability conclude by saying that if men only had charge of things they would go differently. All of which is true, for the very simple reason that men would not, for a single year, suffer the present state of things to continue.

What are the chief difficulties of our present system of domestic service? First, there is the difficulty — and it is a great one in this country, where everybody is born with the belief that one person is just as good as another, and that no one has a right to exercise authority over another — of subordinating servants to the dictates of the individual will. There is an inborn antipathy in them, as in all of us, to being authoritatively directed. Let housekeepers not repine at this; it is in accordance with the spirit of the age to rebel against submission to the dictation of the individual, but to submit cheerfully to the despotism of an organization. But no matter what may be our opinion of the cause, the fact remains that servants grow every year more insubordinate. Second, there is the expense of the system, — board, room, lights, fuel, and waste of servants being a much larger item of expense than their wages. Third, the great variety of work to be done in the house, including work that ought to constitute several distinct departments, as cooking, cleaning, laundry-work, sewing, and caring for children; and fourth, and greatest difficulty of all, the introduction into the family of a foreign element which cannot possibly be assimilated, and which, until it is eliminated wholly, must constantly irritate and injure family life.

But let us not lay the blame for our difficulties on the servants ; they are as little at fault as are the mistresses for the present condition of things. To appreciate things from their standpoint we have only to imagine how it would be if the reverses of fortune, such as we witness with painful frequency in our own day, should bring a beloved child to the necessity of becoming a domestic servant in order to earn her bread. Can we not at once realize the laboriousness of the work, the depressing and deteriorating influences of the constant confinement to the monotonous routine of housework, the absence of the privileges of home, the inferiority of the position? There is scarcely a parent who would not prefer death for a gentle and refined daughter to such a life.   Let us, then, be careful not to expect of other people's daughters what we would reject for our own.

There is no idea more frequently broached by superficial thinkers upon the subject than that of the elevation of domestic service by inducing intelligent and well-educated young women to enter upon it who may in some degree become companions in the family.   Even so profound a student of human relations as Bayard Taylor, in " An Impossible Story," describes a family where " Clara " — a large, handsome young woman, becomingly dressed in a blue French merino, who does the cooking for the family — comes in and takes her place at the table, and acts and is treated just as one of the family, and goes with them after tea (it is not stated who washed the dishes) to hear Emerson lecture. The only sensible thing about the story is its name; it is indeed an " Impossible Story." Impossible, because working over a cooking-stove is absolutely incompatible with blue French merino and a calm and cool readiness to sit down at the table and talk about Emerson, or opera, or any other subject. We do not want companionship in household helpers. We want to be relieved by them of menial toil, of sweeping, of scrubbing, of beefsteak-broiling and waffle-baking, and washing soiled clothes, and ironing starched shirts. Companions we wish to choose and have with us only when we desire their company.

What then is the remedy, if indeed there is a remedy, for the present inharmonious condition of things? The remedy, which may seem impossible to many, will gradually be brought about in cities by the entire separation from the home of all helpers except those who care for and teach our children, and who should indeed be our companions ; and when this department of

the care of the home is absolutely relieved
of its menial aspects, we shall find that educated, refined, and intelligent young women
will seek to become our assistants in the
care of our children. Laundry-work and
cooking have no business in our houses at
all ; they should be performed outside and
sent to us by those whose trade it is to organize such work and do it for the public.
Chamber-work could just as well be performed by women who would come in for
the purpose, and who when their work was
done would go to their own places, there
to enjoy the freedom which we cannot
grant them as house-servants, at the same
time relieving housekeepers of the care and
anxiety caused by a sense of their presence.
All this is more than possible in all cities.
Domestic work must be in the main eliminated from the home, must be organized
by those who shall resolve it into several
distinct branches of business and conduct
it on business principles. The organization
and division of labor is the great fact of
the civilization of to-day ; and wise and

fortunate is that housekeeper who, understanding the drift of things, adjusts as
quickly as possible her life and the life of
her family to the new order of things which
is coming with the certainty of fate.

HOUSEHOLD DECORATION.

THE desire to adorn and beautify the home is one of the highest and best instincts of the human heart. The progress of civilization is first from decoration to use, and then from use to beauty. For instance, it is the instinct of savages to decorate. The Indian rejoices in paint and feathers, and beaded moccasins, and strings of bright colored beads; in robes and tent-covers, with pictures rudely drawn and colored. The more civilized man prefers first use and comfort. He will have a house with floors and windows and utensils and furniture, and he cares more for excellence of construction than for ornament in these. Next after use comes the adornment of neatness and cleanliness; after this, in natural order, that of ornamentation.

It has been quite the fashion of late years to speak with scornful disapproval of the stiffly tidy and unbeautiful homes of our ancestors, especially of our New England ancestors. The reaction against such scrupulous neatness, like all other reactions from extremes, has gone too far, and in our eagerness to banish stiffness from our homes and to introduce artistic variety we are in danger of introducing also very inartistic disorder.

The main distinction between the life of savagery and the life of civilization is that the savage is noisy and uncleanly, the civilized man is quiet and cleanly. The measure of any family's advance in refinement can be taken almost unerringly by an observation on these points. A noisy family is sure to be an uncultivated family, — the noisier the more uncultivated, and the more uncultivated the more untidy and disorderly.

Among the very first elements of household decoration should be named order and tidiness. " Order is heaven's first law ; " and order, system, neatness, and tidiness are the necessary foundation without which no superstructure of decoration or beauty can be reared. Hence it follows that all attempts at household decoration which result simply in the production of articles that must necessarily be easily defaced by use or wear or dust, are futile and false in principle. The home is, first of all, for use and comfort. Chairs are made to sit in, beds and couches are to rest on, windows are to look out of; and any household decoration which interferes with the natural uses of these articles of furniture produces an effect the reverse of pleasant. A pretty and substantial tidy fastened securely on a chair or pillow will produce a pleasant impression. A futile little patch of lace or worsted work or color tacked on in such a manner that it is displaced the moment it is touched, certainly produces a very unpleasant impression. A mass of curtains that effectually prevents a window from being used for the purpose for which it is intended, certainly defeats one of the main objects of household decoration, which is to afford pleasure to the sight.

It might perhaps be laid down as a rule that household decorations that imply the necessity of too much care, or that easily

become marred or defaced, cannot produce a pleasant or restful impression; and
a restful impression is certainly necessary
in order to make beauty enjoyable. Often
the first impression on entering a parlor
or a room all filled up with carved or
embroidered or ornamented articles, or
darkened with hangings and curtains, is
that of weariness as one realizes the immense amount of work and care necessary
to keep them "just so." And if they are
not kept fresh and free from dust, they soon
become offensive to the eye. Is there any
more disagreeable impression than that
made by a room full of rich but neglected
furniture, — dust in the crevices, dust in
the upholstering, dust on the carved brack-
ets and gilded frames, dinginess on the
curtains, and lack of freshness and life
everywhere?

Give us in preference such household
decorations as will either bear the frequent
renovating which use requires, or give us
those which in their very nature are ephemeral. A fresh bouquet of flowers is always beautiful; a withering one is always

ugly. Wreaths and festoons of autumn leaves may be very beautiful and artistic until they begin to be dusty and drooping; then they are always a positive disfigurement. Nothing can produce a permanently pleasant effect in household decoration that does not give an impression of permanence, and of being consistent with the use for which it is intended. All considerations of form, color, contrast, combination, come as an after consideration to those of neatness, permanence, and use.

After these, the next thing to be considered is harmony between a room and its various articles of furniture and adornment. A very plainly-finished low-ceilinged room should not have costly and expensive furniture and carpets and curtains, such as would only befit a spacious mansion. Furniture that is disproportionate in size to a room always makes an unpleasant impression. This is the especial fault of our modern bedroom furniture. There should not be a great disparity of quality in the furniture and adornments of a room. Fine upholstered furniture, lace curtains, and a

rag carpet do not go well together. This
is nothing to the discredit of a rag carpet,
for some of the most delightful and har-
moniously furnished and restful rooms we
have ever seen have been furnished with
a rag carpet, but the pleasant impression
produced was because all things — curtains,
chairs, bookcase, table-cover, chintz-covered
lounge, and rocking-chair — corresponded
and harmonized with the room and with
each other. In such a room yellow muslin
or chintz curtains are beautiful and appropriate, while in other rooms where they
do not harmonize they are simply an eye-
sore and a vexation to the spirit. In such
a room the pretty unframed chromo may
be an adornment to the walls, while the
same chromo in a gilded frame would be
a positive disfigurement in a well furnished
parlor.

No house can be artistically furnished
where the intention of decorating and
adorning is obtrusively obvious. " The
highest aim of art is to conceal art." An
over-ornamented house and an over-dressed
woman produce the same effect upon the

observer; they both express an essentially uncultivated taste. All household decorations should have some good " excuse for being; " and the quantities of carved and embroidered and ornamented things which fill up and crowd many modern houses are simply manifestations of an uncultured and misdirected activity on the part of those who are responsible for them. " Nothing in excess," was a fundamental rule in Greek art. It is one of the most essential fundamental rules in artistic household decoration.

MOTHERS-IN-LAW.

NO class of women in society has been so unjustly ridiculed and made the butt of cheap wit as mothers-in-law. To such an extent has this been carried that young wives and young husbands have learned to regard the mother-in-law with suspicion and distrust from the very outset, and to repel the least manifestation of kindness and interest on the part of her who holds this relation as an unwarrantable interference and intrusion. Many a kind mother's heart has been pained by such treatment, when nothing was further from her intention than to interfere in the wedded affairs of her children; and many a young couple are by this injurious prejudice deprived of the inestimable advantages that may come to young married people through the possession of a kind and wise mother-in-law.

Of course there are mothers-in-law, as there are women in every relation of life, who are meddlesome, suspicious, fault-finding, and hard to get along with; but observation shows that such are not in the majority. And while the disagreeable peculiarities of troublesome mothers-in-law have been exaggerated, caricatured, and generalized, until they, as a class, are made to bear the odium that should attach to the few, it is rare indeed to find their virtues recorded and their praises sounded, or their true and honorable and useful place in society recognized.

A beautiful and talented woman, who was the mother of several children, and who became the victim of ill health, once said, speaking of her husband's mother, who had come to live with her: "Every married woman who has little children to care for and train needs a woman for a companion. None but a sympathizing friend of her own sex can give her the help and encouragement and counsel that she needs." The truth of this sentiment many a young mother and housekeeper will recognize.

Only a woman can understand a woman's needs, aches, disappointments, cares, and daily trials generally; and happy is that wife and mother who finds such a friend and companion in her mother-in-law or in her mother. Half the cares and perplexities of married life and of rearing a family of children may be lifted by such kind, loving, and sympathizing companionship.

In the first place, in regard to household cares alone, how valuable is the kindly given and kindly taken advice of the experienced mother-in-law! She knows all the ins and outs of housekeeping. She is familiar with all the mysteries of baking, preserving, pickling, and all those little arts of fine housekeeping which the young housekeeper generally has to learn by experience. She can tell just how to put away jellies and preserves and canned fruits so that they will not spoil; she can tell just the reason why the bread did not rise or the pastry is heavy; and the heeding of a word of instruction from her on these points may save the young housekeeper many a perplexity, if only she will cherish a kind and docile spirit in such matters. Many a young housekeeper, however, deprives herself of all such advantages by refusing to admit that she can be instructed in anything, and in so doing she wounds and pains a heart that would have rejoiced to be of use to her; and were a little deference shown, it would have insured the most perfect harmony. Then for all the little mishaps of housekeeping the kind mother-in-law has an ever-ready panacea. "Do not mind it; do not fret; such accidents will happen in all household matters; it is really of trifling importance, and the only way to do is to forget it and try to succeed better next time."

But it is where the care of little children is concerned that the good mother-in-law shines in her brightest and best light. No house that has a baby in it is complete without a grandma; and happy is that baby, and happy is that young mother who possesses one. The whole care of a young babe is too much for any mother, especially if it is her first one; and this care cannot be rightly shared with one who is irresponsible, as children's nurses too often are. None but young mothers who have been compelled to take the whole care of an infant can ever know the exhausting weariness that results from it. It is injurious both to the child and the mother. The child needs a change of care, so that it may not always be acted upon by the same influences; and the mother needs, at times, absolute respite from care, both for her mental and bodily health. To render the needed assistance no one on earth is equal to the good mother-in-law. She probably loves the little one as well as if it were her own child; and when it is in her loving arms or under her gentle care, the mother may go free for a little, thus rejuvenating her health and spirits, and making her what she ought to be, cheerful and happy.

And as a permanent member of a family, who so useful, so prized, and rightfully so happy as the mother-in-law? Relieved of the heavier and more absorbing cares of the household, she has time and inclination to be a helper to every one. She may be the one member of the family who may do more

to make household affairs run smoothly
than any other. In every family there are
so many little things needed to be done
that tax time and patience, and yet that left
undone breed inconvenience and discomfort. There is the little stitch of mending
to be done on the clean clothes, the missing
button to be replaced, the starting hole in
the stocking to be circumvented; there is
the doll dress to be made, and the ball to
be covered, and the mittens to be knit.
Indeed, a family of children who do not
know a kind grandmother's care have
missed a great deal in life.

And what more beautiful sight on earth
than to see a grandmother surrounded by
loving little hearts, and clung to by tender
though often troublesome little hands?
And while it is always sad to see a grandmother really burdened with cares for her
grandchildren, yet in a right condition of
society and family life there is no more
beautiful and happiness-giving and useful
relation than that of grandmother or
mother-in-law, nor one that should be
treated with more honor and affection.

HOME-MAKING AS A PROFESSION FOR WOMEN.

THE multiplication of cooking-schools in large cities and towns, and the popularity and success of courses of lectures on the art of cooking before large private classes of ladies, are significant signs of social progress. In the case of lectures on the art of cooking, it is conclusively proven that they are becoming both popular and fashionable, by the fact that many of our best seminaries for young ladies include in their curriculum a course of lectures on the subject. Doubtless the young ladies who listen to these lectures, note-book in hand, will learn a great many useful facts in regard to the preparation of food, though we all recognize the truth that it will require practice and experience in the work of cooking to make their knowledge available. In the case of cooking-schools, it seems to be a mooted question whether the schools should be for housekeepers who employ cooks, or for those who are employed as cooks.

As cooking develops into an art, or a special occupation, it tends to separation from all other work. This is in accordance with the laws of industrial organization. The first-class, well-trained or professional cook does not want to, and will not, wash the dishes or do any other work. Just here is where the difficulty is going to prove the greatest in the way of private families of moderate means securing good cooks. The really good cook now-a-days can get high wages for doing cooking and nothing else, either in wealthy private families or in hotels and boarding-houses. Just as soon as a smart, intelligent domestic acquires thoroughly the art of cooking, she is in such demand and can command such prices for her work as removes her beyond the reach of employment by people of moderate incomes ; and the higher the wages the easier the place as a general rule. The fact is a truly discouraging one to those among housekeepers who have hoped the cooking-school was going to help solve the vexed domestic-service problem.

The question will however, we think, be much helped toward solution by the multiplication of cooking-schools. The training of cooks will have the effect of raising their wages beyond the reach of people of moderate incomes. Eventually families who cannot afford to keep high-priced cooks will find some other mode of procuring their meals. Many experiments are now being made, both by families and inventors, which have for their object the discovery of how families may have their meals provided for them without the expense and care of the individual kitchen. And out of the general agitation and discussion of the whole question, and as a result of the urgent needs of society, we hope to see arise among women a new professional class, — home-makers.

But is not this the boarding-house keeper under a new name; and are not the terms " boarding-house " and " boarding-house keeper" synonyms for discomfort and shabby economies, for antagonism and inharmony? Can a boarding-house ever be made a home?

Most assuredly, provided that the proper directing spirit is at the head of it, and provided also that houses used for the purpose are built so as to be adapted to the use indicated. Scarcely anything could be imagined more uncomfortable for the accommodation of a number of people under one roof than the ordinary city house. In order to have the kind of homes which professional home-makers would make successful, buildings especially designed for the purpose must be erected. The buildings known as "flats" are an approach toward the kind of houses that would be needed. Elevators — the last best gift of the inventive genius of man to advancing civilization — will help solve the problem. Our "homes" must be so planned that every family or every individual can preserve a distinct individuality, and yet have a common meeting-ground if desired. The home-maker would probably reserve for her own use the highest floor, and on this floor should be the dining-room and kitchen. She should be a woman of such intelligence, dignity, and spirit as to be able to organize and guide the household, which should be composed of those who, in her judgment, would at least not be uncongenial. The successful home-maker would probably be able to draw around her such a congenial circle as would make possible association with those under her roof a pleasure and an honor to be sought after. She would have capital enough to enable her to provide everything for the comfort of those who became her patrons, and she should charge such prices as would remunerate her well for the work of making a home for them. Under her roof would be found families; young men and women, all provided with the comforts of home. The association of so many together would enable the home-keeper to develop her work into departments; the trained cook would enable her to furnish better food than the unskilled servant in the individual kitchen could possibly do; and a new institution in city life would help solve some of the difficulties experienced by people in finding or making homes. In this profession, under proper conditions, many a noble single woman or dependent widow, now groaning in spirit under the infliction of enforced inaction, or perhaps toiling at some unsuitable, uncongenial, and unremunerative occupation, would find a rewarding and influential work.   The multiplication and development of such homes in cities could not fail to be a great social blessing.

TWO TYPES OF WOMEN.

I.

THE WOMAN WHO CAN TAKE CARE OF HERSELF.

"WHAT a blessing and what a relief to find a woman who can take care of herself!" The remark fell from the lips of a beautiful matron, richly dressed and surrounded by every appurtenance of wealth and luxury. She was president of an association of women whose object was to aid their own sex in obtaining employment, and to assist them in straits of any kind. As part of their machinery, they had an employment bureau. The cause of the exclamation above quoted was that a self-possessed but by no means handsome young woman had called the day before and asked permission to look over their employment list. She stated that she was a stranger in the city, had but little money, and that she wanted employment as soon as possible.

There was, however, no whining, no complaint, no apprehension expressed, nor aid asked further than to obtain the desired information as to vacant situations. Making a note of an advertisement for a female book-compositor, a governess for a small family, and a forewoman in a millinery store, she departed. The next day she returned and stated that she had secured the situation as governess. The ladies were somewhat surprised, as many applicants had tried for it, but for some reason or other no engagement had ever been effected. In explanation, the young lady said that the place was evidently a hard one, the wages low, and the duties exacting ; " but," said she cheerfully, " I will take it and do the best I can, till I get something better. I am sure I shall soon find just the employment I want ; I am used to taking care of myself."

The expression of confidence in her own ability to take care of herself was made so earnestly and yet so modestly, and was withal such a pleasing change from the manner of most applicants for employment or assistance, that the lady managers were much impressed, and mentally made a note that the young lady would be sure to succeed at almost anything. The majority of those who applied to these good ladies seemed to feel that the most becoming attitude in which feminine nature could appear was the attitude of helplessness. To assert that they had never been used to doing anything, that they had seen better days, and to recount with tears the misfortunes of their lives, was the most general way of introducing themselves. The secretary of the society, an energetic maiden lady of fifty years or over, was wont to declare that the whole race of employment-seekers among women might be described under the title "The Woman who Cries;" and she was also emphatic in her conclusion that until a woman got over the weakness of tears in connection with her search for employment, there was but little hope for her. Obtaining employment is a pure matter of business, — so much service for so much pay; and pride and grief and tears are entirely foreign to the question.

It is probable that a large part of this supersensitiveness among women who look for employment arises from the fact that they think that women who can take care of themselves are not as much admired and respected by men as those who are really or affectedly helpless and dependent. Nothing could be farther from the truth. The woman who is sufficient unto herself; who goes where she lists and employs her talents at whatsoever she likes; who takes an honest pride in earning and handling her own money; who keeps her business to herself and asks neither advice nor assistance,—she is the one who really secures the admiration and respect of all men whose respect is worth having. Grace Greenwood says she has always observed that upon the ocean every man respects and admires and commends the woman who can swim. So, too, do all sensible women. Times are greatly changing; whether they will or not, women are thrown out into the waves, and must swim or drown in the stormy sea of life. There is no use fretting about it; there is, indeed, no time even to discuss the question; preconceived ideas of the proprieties of life, woman's sphere, and all that, have to stand aside; the question is bread, bread. And such being the case, the most admirable and encouraging person that one can possibly meet in these latter days is the woman who can take care of herself.

II.

THE WOMAN WHO OUGHT TO BE CARED FOR.

THE woman who, when circumstances require it can take care of herself, is a truly admirable and delightful person to meet. She encourages our hearts to hope that our daughters may be fitted by proper education to meet the emergencies of life cheerfully, bravely, and successfully. But it is probable that we all feel, when planning for the future of our daughters, that if they are called upon to fulfil the whole of woman's natural destiny, if they become wives and mothers, their normal condition, and that which would be the most favorable to their own happiness and complete and harmonious development, would be that of being cared for. In this condition, as in all proper conditions, they are entitled to all the rights and privileges, and have all the claims upon the respect and kindness of men, that could possibly be claimed or awarded to the most enterprising and successful workers among women in any department of the world's work.

A distinguished politician once said that women have all the rights men have, and one more, — the right of being protected. In this statement he showed his discrimination and genuine politeness, in that he did not use the common phraseology and say the right of being supported. A man has no more business to say he supports his wife than he has to say he supports his partner or his clerks. All good wives render a full *quid pro quo* in the partnership of the home, even though they do nothing but make home pleasant and meet their husbands on their return from business with a smile. A young woman, by virtue of a fine education and natural abilities, is able as a teacher to earn, say, a thousand dollars a year. A young fellow asks her to relinquish this and join him in founding a home, her part in it being, perhaps, mainly to stay in the house and overlook the housekeeping. She may consent to do so, with most happy results both to herself and him; but one essential element in her happiness must be that by so doing she does not place herself in a position that shall create a painful sense of dependence. There is no high-spirited woman who can endure without pain such a position; yet there is no rightly constituted woman who under the right conditions does not enjoy having all her temporal wants supplied and being cared for and protected.

An earnest and thoughtful writer upon social questions of the deepest importance says that what this country most needs is a leisurely, happy, and care-free motherhood. The period when a mother has her little ones around her knees ought to be the happiest of her life. But when maternal cares press, a stronger hand than hers should ward off all other cares and trials that would oppress her or interfere with her care for her children. This is the period when woman's most sacred right is that of being cared for and protected. Alas, that to so many mothers the period of maternity is one of being overburdened physically and mentally, and of unrest and sorrow of spirit! And this condition is one from which, in a majority of cases, she cannot rescue herself. She may need recreation, change, help in her labors, and many other things essential to a healthful condition of mind and body; but she lacks the strength and energy to provide herself with them. Here is the opportunity for the good husband. Here is his chance to bind his wife to him with "hooks of steel;" here is his time to show that he appreciates what is due to woman in the most important relations of life. But in order to do this he must render this homage not as one who gives to a dependent, but rather as one who brings glad tribute to a sacred altar.

HEALTH FOR WOMEN.

FRANCES POWER COBBE, whose writings we heartily wish were better known to the women of this country, once wrote an article entitled " The Little Health of Women," which was so widely copied by the best American newspapers as to indicate that the sentiments expressed excited interest and attention. This lady, who can never be accused of writing anything trifling, states carefully what she believes to be the causes of valetudinarianism among women. First among these she places excessive draughts upon the nervous and emotional nature of women through a false view of their duties to their families. She instances their blind devotion in sickness or misfortune, which causes them to sacrifice sleep, food, and rest, to the ultimate greater loss of those who have claims upon them. After enumerating various other causes, she discusses dress as related to health, and finally occupation. One cause of little health she briefly adverts to in these words : " Another source of *petite santé*, I fear, may be found resulting from a lingering survival among us of the idiotic notion that there is something particularly ' lady-like ' in invalidism, pallor, small appetite, and a languid mode of speech and manners. The very word ' delicacy,' properly a term of praise, being applied vulgarly to a valetudinary condition, is evidence that the impression of the dandies of sixty years ago, that refinement and sickness were convertible terms, is not yet wholly exploded." Thus arose, and lingers yet, the fashion of being weak and timid and clinging. In the days of chivalry the lover's chief attribute was his power of protection ; the lady's chief desire, to be protected. When she no longer needed to be protected from the rudeness of war, an imaginary danger must be found to be guarded against. The rude wind of heaven must not blow too rudely on the fair maiden ; and when there was absolutely no personal danger to her from anything, a

simulated weakness of body must be sub-
stituted so that the lover could at least
have the pleasure of protecting her against
herself.

In other and plainer words, it has been
fashionable in days past, if it is not now,
to be " delicate ; " and one of the most efficient means that could be used to make
women healthy would be to make health
fashionable. In accomplishing this result,
as is always the case when any great hu-
manitarian project is on hand, the efficient
co-operation and encouragement of men
will be required to accomplish successfully
the end desired.

The philosophy of the power of fashion
over men and women, but more especially
over women, is probably not yet fully
understood. Especially is it an enigma
why fashionably dressed women, no matter
how extravagant and unnatural their style
of dress, generally receive the most attention from gentlemen, and appear to be the
most attractive to them. Many a young
girl who would prefer to dress sensibly and
healthfully is deterred from doing so by

the fact that she would thereby be marked as strong-minded, and avoided by gentlemen. Perhaps it is because one of the best natural sentiments is the desire to be attractive to the opposite sex, and girls who dress to attract attention only have this naturally correct sentiment developed in excess. For the time being, it generally secures its object; and no complaint is more common or well founded than that gentle men are attracted to such rather than to the plainly dressed girl who thinks of something else beside dress and beaux.

As a sign of a healthier sentiment which is beginning to prevail, and which openly expressed by men would do more to make women aim to be healthy than volumes of disquisitions on dress and food, we note the expression of a gentleman in speaking of a young lady in whose efforts to obtain an artistic education he was much interested. He said: "I very much admire the energy and ability of that young lady, but I could never love her; she looks too unhealthy." Now, this very same young lady rather felt that her pale cheeks, dark-circled eyes, cold hands, and willowy form were elements of attractiveness; that a description of them would read well in a novel. She resisted all importunities of her teachers to adapt her dress to her work, so that it should not weary her by its pressure upon vital organs. She daily dragged a long heavy skirt around, the while lamenting that it nearly killed her. [Could she but realize that her unhealthy appearance was really repulsive instead of attractive] how quickly would her corsets be loosened, her skirts lightened and shortened, and exercise and baths and abundant food be resorted to in order to acquire the attractiveness of health!

For health is not only beauty, but it is the only possible preservative of beauty. Health for women has been long enough preached, and widely enough sought in the last twenty-five years, to give us some of the rarest specimens of beauty in women not only preserved but greatly enhanced in middle life and old age. We meet women in society, who are the mothers of grown daughters, whose peachy complexions, sound teeth, and plump, soft faces show the power of health to defy time itself. In olden days a woman who retained her beauty past the age of forty years was considered a marvel. A few names, such as those of Ninon de l'Enclos, Madame Récamier, and others, have been made famous chiefly by the remarkable preservation of their beauty. We may be sure the chief element in its preservation was health. No complexion artificially made by cosmetics will stand the test of age. Wrinkles are inevitable if the digestive organs do not act vigorously. To adapt the saying of Marcus Aurelius, "The aids to noble life are all within," we might truthfully say, the aids to health and beauty are all contained within the wondrous organism of the body, and conditioned upon their proper exercise.

We have great hopes from the present indications that health and healthful styles of dress are soon to be made fashionable. The short walking-dresses, the large, gracefully proportioned waists, the loose street garments; the broad, solid, easy, low-heeled shoes now seen in the windows of the best shoe-dealers; the return to a simpler fashion of wearing the hair, and the discarding of the hurtful chignon, — all of these point to the coming of a day when to be in perfect health will be indispensable to being in perfect fashion.

THE SUPERIOR WOMAN.

IT is curious, when we think of it, to note the prevalence of the phrase, "a superior woman," as used to describe unusually good, intelligent, or useful women, when such an expression as "a superior man" would produce an impression of surprise or oddity. There is something in the expression which implies that women generally are not superior, and that one of this description is rather exceptional. When we hear the phrase the force of contrast brings to our minds the characteristics of women who are inferior; and probably the chief distinction of the really superior woman consists in her freedom from the follies, weaknesses, littlenesses, and trifling aims of womankind, rather than in her actual acquirements.

For the superior woman is found in every class and condition of society. Her chief characteristic, and one that must be a basis for her whole course of life, is a knowledge and an appreciation of the proper relations of things, or what Hamerton would call just thinking. Hence trifles never assume in her eyes the importance of principles. That women are too easily impressed and disconcerted and thrown off their balance by trifles, has been the complaint against them from time immemorial, and not without cause. Their education and the narrow range of their interests have been to blame for this in times past; but things are changing. Woman is no longer compelled to walk along the monotonous levels of life with her duties as sand about her feet; to her it is given now to rise to the mountain heights of thought or achievement; and the results upon her character are every day becoming more apparent.

The superior woman always has large philanthropy. Not that factitious, uneasy sentiment which expends itself in church festivals or sewing societies or charity balls, but that which regulates all her intercourse with society. Hence she is never found ready to impute wrong motives to people; never ready and eager to cry down the wayward and guilty. Nor will she ever be found among the narrow-minded class of puritanical spirits who, perhaps without capacity for temptation, or knowledge of life wide enough to enable them to estimate its power, would forever shut the door in the face of one who has done wrong. Rather she will be ready to believe that the very fact of wrong-doing, and suffering the sting it carries with it, may give an impulse to a nobler and better life than ever. Hence the superior woman naturally attracts to herself struggling and repenting souls; and her broad charity, which believeth all things and hopeth all things, is a constant stimulus to them in their efforts after better things.

As a member of society the superior woman is wholly above gossip. This does not necessarily mean an indifference to, or a lack of interest in, the lives, actions, and doings of our neighbors. The essence of gossip in its mischievous sense is the repeating of remarks or criticisms or the relation of incidents calculated to make divisions and hard feelings between friends and acquaintances. Nothing but the most serious considerations will ever justify the repetition to one friend of the unkind or derogatory remarks made by another, and yet this is an offence of which women are too often guilty. We all have our annoyances and troubles, and it is often a great relief and help to disburden them to a friendly ear. We even like to make our complaints of the conduct and treatment of friends; but if we pour them into an ear that listens but to repeat, we are indeed sowing sorrow and trouble for ourselves. But when we have a friend in the superior woman we know that such confidences are sacred; we feel that her calm judgment and clear insight will help us to judge rightly of things which on account of their nearness and annoying nature we are unable to estimate justly. What a privilege to have a friend in whose honor we can trust, and whose sense of right will even restrain and direct us if we are likely to be hasty in our judgments or too rash in our actions!

" Speech is silver, but silence is golden," says the old proverb, and it is exemplified in the case of the superior woman. What an immense advantage is possessed by the person who can keep silence ! The thought once spoken is forever after our master ; we are its slave. In no one thing in the conduct of life is superiority of character more displayed than in the control of speech.

But no atmosphere of superior sanctity or self-conscious rectitude or dignity surrounds the superior woman. She is as accessible as the sunlight, and like the sun she shines upon the evil and the good. Her presence is an encouragement to every noble purpose, as her character and conduct are an example for all who would rise above the pettiness of life. Her heart is a fountain of love for humanity ; her strength of character and just estimate of life are a tower of strength in all seasons of perplexity and doubt.

THE NEW OLD AGE.

A VERY singular trial, lately closed in London, reveals the strange fact that there are persons in this enlightened age who believe that there is a possibility of defying the ravages of age and retaining the comely looks of youth by means of certain potions and cosmetics. A daughter of the celebrated singer Mario fell into the toils of a Madame Rachel, an "Arabian Perfumer," who, for the consideration of £200, agreed to furnish her with washes and cosmetics that would preserve the beauty of twenty until she was sixty. The cosmetics, instead of beautifying the lady's complexion, caused it to break out with a dreadful humor. Her anxiety was appeased by Madame Rachel, who told her that this was a necessary part of the beautifying process, but that she needed additional washes. To pay for these the lady placed her jewels in the hands of the impostor, who speedily placed them in pawn. Finally the unfortunate lady, driven to desperation by her disfigured face, and by seeing her jewels publicly exposed, summoned courage to tell her husband, who at once had the "Arabian Perfumer" arrested. She was tried and justly sentenced to five years' solitary imprisonment.

But if some may be found who seek to preserve the charms of youth by artificial processes, a far greater number realize that in many respects old age is not dreaded as it once was, especially by women. We have learned that the new old age may possess charms surpassing even those of youth. Many matrons of to-day are at forty far more beautiful than they were at twenty. Not only in face and form are beauty and attractiveness increased, but mental charms increase correspondingly. Where can be found a more entertaining companion than the sensible woman whose sympathies with life are fresh and tender, whose judgment is matured, whose experience is wide, whose observation is trained, and from whose conversation frivolity and affectation flee ?

And what a rich and wide sphere of enjoyment opens up before the educated women of to-day who have . passed the boundaries of youth and reached the prime and vigor of life! With domestic duties for the most part fulfilled, with her children trained to usefulness and gone out to take their own part in the world's work, the mind of the happy matron, enriched by the experiences of motherhood and strengthened by a genuine sympathy with every human interest, goes forth to a new world of work and reward. Every human interest is hers,—to look after the poor and suffering, to help on every benevolent project, to take an interest in schools, to study the principles that should govern all charitable enterprises, to do good to all around her. Among such women are to be found our very best advisers and most efficient helpers in the management of all public institutions for the unfortunate,— the insane, the blind, the deaf and dumb, the inmates of houses of refuge and indus-

trial homes.   Free from all merely personal
ambitions and vanities, they bring to such
work the very best and most unselfish en-
ergies of which the human heart is capable;
and experience has shown that under such
circumstances women have been the most
successful workers in the world.   Mary
Carpenter revolutionized the Irish prisons;
Dorothea Dix aroused an interest in and
ameliorated the condition of the insane all
over the world; Elizabeth Peabody and the
band of noble women she has gathered
around her have engrafted the kinder-
garten on the American school system;
and innumerable benevolent organizations
all over the country by their efficiency and
success testify to the cheerful, effective
work of good women.   The field widens
every day; opportunities multiply and
broaden.   There is a constantly increasing
demand for the service of humanity that
can best be rendered by mature, intelligent, dignified, noble women.   By this fact
women are constantly reminded that mature years will not diminish, but rather
increase, their interest in life, and bring

honor, opportunity, respect, and satisfying work.

And this new old age needs no artificial aids to preserve even physical beauty. Attention to the laws of health is the only necessary preservative and beautifier. Gray hair has established its claim to beauty whenever Nature whitens it. The teeth, if cared for properly from early youth, need never show decay; and if they do, dental science affords an excellent remedy. Exercise will give vigor to the step and preserve the erectness of the frame. A kind heart and a gentle disposition will pencil lines of beauty in the countenance. Indeed, many a face that was homely in youth, under the influence of time and generous and happy impulses, becomes really beautiful in old age. The complexion mellows, the eye brightens, the smile softens, and a beauty born of a lofty nature shines out more and more brightly in the face.

And so while heretofore it has seemed to be the especial privilege of manhood to increase in dignity, honor, and usefulness with age, the new old age for women holds

out equally fair gifts and satisfying honors.
All that youth prizes of comeliness, pleasure, and interest in life are still hers;
and in addition is offered the contentment
of mind that comes from a sense of useful and rewarding occupation, of increasing knowledge, and of hopeful progress
toward the goal of a happy and perfected
humanity.

ONE of the most significant facts of modern social organization, especially in America, is the growth and widespread social fashion of Women's Clubs. It is but a few years since women living in less favored localities heard with a kind of admiring awe of the Sorosis, — a club formed by a select and favored few of the opulent and literary women of New York; and of the Women's Club of Boston, formed on a somewhat different plan. To aspire to belong to either of these seemed like aspiring to have one's name written high in the scroll of fame. For was not Alice Cary the president of Sorosis, and "Jennie June" an officer of the association? And were not Mrs. Julia Ward Howe, Mrs. Lydia Maria Child, and Mrs. Ednah D. Cheney members of the Boston Women's Club? But little more than half a score of years have passed, and there is scarce a town of any respectable size east or west but has its Women's Club, or maybe half a dozen of them. Their objects are various, but are chiefly literary. They are usually formed, as stated in their constitution and by-laws, for mutual improvement and for the purpose of stimulating and assisting each other in the study of literature, art, science, philanthropy, political or social economy.

That women should combine together at all for any purpose whatever is, however, the most significant fact; and that they should have come to appreciate the benefits of organization and its power to accomplish plans and purposes of their own marks a distinct stage in the development of the intelligence of women and of their influence upon society. We can all of us remember when the only social organization known among women was the sewing-circle and the missionary society. The solemn and unusual duties of president, vice-president, and secretary of such societies gave those elected to these offices a certain distinction not unlike that of being

captain in the old "musters" among men.
Their objects, though worthy, were essentially narrow, and the most common tra-
dition in regard to them is that they were
hot-beds of gossip and neighborhood quarrels. Probably they would long since have
died out except that this was the one activity
of women outside of home that had the countenance and encouragement of the church.
It was at least a relief from the monotony
of getting three meals a day, and of doing
up the spring and fall sewing. But even
in these crude beginnings of association
and organization among women, the power
it gave them soon began to be realized. It
might almost be said that the knowledge of
the power of organization is to women the
modern tree of the knowledge of good and
evil. They have tasted of it, and as a result it seems probable that they will become
as gods, or as men, in their power to effect
their own ends and compel and control
society to their wishes. For an illustration of their effectiveness in missionary
organizations we have only to look at the
hundreds of thousands of dollars raised

annually by women's boards of missions; and for an illustration of their power in controlling society we have only to look at the results of the work of the Women's Christian Temperance Union.

It is not probable, however, that women themselves, in their organization of women's societies and clubs, had any idea of such results as those which will be sure to follow. Rather these clubs had their origin in the desire or the necessity for expression which was the result of the higher education and increased intellectual development of women. Education of any or all the natural faculties prompts to their exercise and expression. For such expression men have always had an opportunity in their social and commercial relations with one another. It is a conceded fact that men, as a class, are happier and more contented than women. There is among them none of that restless self-consciousness, that inquiry and discussion as to the aim of life, that so largely characterizes the womanhood of to-day.

This unconsciousness is the sign of mental health among men, just as this consciousness is a sign of mental unhealth and wrong relations somewhere among women. But this content of men arises from this power to express themselves, this perfect freedom for the exercise of any and every natural gift which they possess by bringing it into the market of the world, and receiving in return for its exercise pecuniary or other reward. Women have been restricted in the expression of their faculties to a few so-called feminine occupations and to the household. To be sure, woman finds in the family room for the expression of her strongest instinct, — the maternal one ; but there are others that also require expression. The cry of the educated woman of to-day is the cry of the active child, and it is the expression of the same eternal necessity of the developing intellectual nature, — "*I want to do something.*"

And since men took no particular notice of this need and desire of women for expression, or if they did only frowned upon it as something unwomanly, or treated the complaints which were made as they would treat the restless desires of the unoccupied child ; since they persisted in pronouncing it a misfortune for a woman to enter into the activities of life, or to be obliged by circumstances to bring her capabilities for doing something into the markets of the world, and offering them for money (which is but another name for independence, development, individuality, power, and everything else that makes life desirable), — we find that the activities of women are finding another outlet, and it may be with results little dreamed of at present. Women's clubs are discussing the public-school systems ; they are comparing notes on the education of their children ; they are scrutinizing and passing upon the qualifications of teachers. Realizing their great common interest in the schools, they are beginning to inquire into the way school boards are chosen, and the question is mooted in their clubs whether women should not have a voice in choosing the members of the school boards, or in fact whether it would not be a good thing to have a few of their own sex placed on such boards.

Women are discussing in their club meetings the temperance question, and are pondering upon the reply once made by the Mayor of Chicago to the thousands of mothers who petitioned him to enforce the law against selling liquor to minors. He said, in substance : " Ladies, you do not form any part of our constituency, and we are here for the purpose of enforcing the will of our constituents." They are reflecting on the meaning of the word " constituency " in a country like ours, and discussing the question whether it would or would not be a good thing for women to form a part of the constituency of the powers that be in the government of a city, at least in temperance and school questions. They are studying up on philosophy ; they are becoming intelligently interested in the labor question ; they are reading history together ; they are studying the principles of art ; in fact, women's clubs are generating and stimulating an amount of intellectual activity among women that must eventually tell powerfully upon society at large.

Many other things women are learning

in their clubs. For one thing, they are
nearly all conducted according to strict par-
liamentary forms; and through obedience
to these, women are learning to respect the
opinions of others at the same time that
they are learning to maintain and express
their own. They are acquiring self-posses-
sion and power in expressing their thoughts;
and the very fact and act of expressing
thought tends to make them more careful
thinkers, and to make them weigh and be
exact in their statements. They are also
learning the happy stimulus which is given
to all human progress by association for
a common end. Herein they discern the
reason why so much of woman's education
seems to fall fruitless to the earth and
ceases to progress after school-days are
ended. It is because there is lacking the
incentive of achievement. Very few progress so far during school-days as to learn
to love study for its own sake. They remember, however, that they did enjoy and
love study when the incentive was meeting
with their schoolmates and reciting to their
teachers. They now observe that while to

read carefully and make an intelligent sy-
nopsis of some book would be a work of
no interest if done simply for one's own
improvement (as teachers say), yet it becomes a work of delightful interest when
it is done for a club meeting. In this fact
is a suggestion as to the reason why so
many girls who study music cease to take
interest in it when they do not have the
stimulus of taking lessons. It is perhaps
one of the wise provisions of Providence
for binding the human race together, that
we cannot enjoy any acquirement or pleasure alone, — that we must share it. As a
certain speculative philosopher has shown
us, all spiritual treasures are increased by
being shared. All true incentive toward
human progress, which is the aggregate of
individual progress, comes from association
with one another. Even those who seem
to work alone are no exception to this rule.
The musician at his instrument, composing
and giving form to the harmonies that fill
his brain, is happy in his work because he
is creating that which shall exist apart
from himself; the philosopher or student

of science, seemingly toiling alone, is dis-
covering and formulating principles which
shall be recognized and appropriated by his
fellow-beings, and in this consciousness he
finds his happiest stimulus.

And thus it will come to pass that women's clubs as organizations will come to
partake of this nature of the individuals
who compose them; they will not long be
content to centre their action upon themselves. They will not long meet and study
and discuss subjects simply for mutual improvement. They will seek methods of
applying the truths they perceive, the principles they discover, to objects and ends
outside of themselves. This result may not
be foreseen by those now most interested
and active in women's clubs, but it is inevitable; otherwise they will run their little
round of being and cease to exist. There
is already a movement on the part of the
more vigorous women's clubs to get into
communication with one another for purposes of mutual interest. Consider what a
vast force in moulding public opinion on any
subject, the united action of such organiza-

tions all over the country would possess. The thousands of individual clubs are the nerve centres where spiritual and intellectual life is generated; and when once these are placed in vital communication with each other we shall have a great controlling brain power through the larger organization, whose action upon society none can as yet foresee, but which gives the noblest promise of good. For it will represent, as has never been represented before, the conservative maternal element of human nature. We may, above all things, be sure that "whatsoever things are honest, whatsoever things are pure, whatsoever things are lovely, whatsoever things are of good report," the members of the women's clubs throughout the country will "think on these things."

UNFINISHED WORK.

IN her noble and inspiring book, "The Hopes of the Human Race," Frances Power Cobbe presents one of the most powerful arguments ever written in favor of a belief in immortality. She bases her argument wholly upon the expectation of justice. She says that for all wrongs, all bereavements, all disappointments, the human soul can find consolation so long as it believes that in the end all things will be justly recompensed. So long as the soul triumphantly answers in the affirmative the question of Abraham in his agony, "Shall not the Judge of all the earth do right?" it has an anchor to cling to. But once let the doubt or belief that justice will fail enter the soul, and every moral intuition withers, the moral law ceases to have any meaning, there is no such thing as right and wrong, and the universe is a fraud.

There is another argument which must be almost equally powerful to those who are interested in and closely observe the moral forces at work in society. It is the argument of unfinished work; of unaccomplished desires for the good of the human race; of aspirations that have never even found expression; of ideals that have never been realized; of benevolent feelings that have never found play; of ability and power to do good that have never known opportunity. There is really a vast amount of moral force, of that precious "directive power," latent in society, but it seems to find no adequate means of expression. It appears to waste itself beating the air. Can it be that all this is lost? Is there not in the moral world a law corresponding to the law of the Correlation of Forces in the material world, and which assures us that no force is ever lost out of the universe; that it continually translates itself into other forms of force, and in the economy of the Creator does its appointed work?

This question becomes especially interesting when considered in relation to the work, the wishes, the hopes, the necessities, the aspirations and efforts of women. The Church has long recognized how much of its power for good lay in the women of its membership; and the permission and encouragement given them within the past few years to enter upon the great benevolent projects of the Church, through regularly organized associations, is a significant fact in the progress of the world. The Church knows that it can depend upon women for their time, their strength, their money, in so far as they control it, and for the most unlimited self-denial. But these church organizations, after all, give but small scope to the vast latent moral force that waits but for favorable opportunities for development among good and educated women everywhere. There are other and greater changes needed in the organization of society before the moral power of women can have its full effect, before their hopes for the welfare of humanity can be realized, before their efforts can be made effective in any practical way.

At the present time the harvest is ripe

and great; the laborers are not few, but they have no sickles, and small and ineffectual is the amount they can reap with their hands. Here is really the problem of the hour, to bring the work and the workers together. Who will organize the work and the workers? It is really pathetic to look abroad in society and see so much work that needs to be done that is left undone, and then on the other hand to see thousands of noble and good workers eager and anxious to do the work could they but be brought into a position to do it. Scores and hundreds of intelligent, benevolent-hearted women have read and are reading with intense interest the able articles on the best methods of improving the conditions of society, which have of late years been so marked a feature of our best magazines and reviews. They have felt their hearts glow with the "enthusiasm of humanity," and the patriotic and noble inspiration to lend a hand and be a part of the working power for uplifting the world. The only question has been how to find adequate and worthy opportunity.

In connection with such thoughts, women ought to consider the following facts. The fundamental principle of our civilization is the division of labor; its most significant fact is the growth of cities. The world's work has ceased to be distinctively classified into masculine and feminine. The spirit of industrial organization has already taken nearly all former feminine handicrafts out of the home, and on the other hand has drawn women from the home to make them a part of the industrial organization of the world. As in the industrial world little can now be accomplished by the puny efforts of the individual; as all effort, to be effective, must be so through the regularly organized machinery of manufacture and commerce: so in the work to be done for the elevation and renovation of society, little can be done by the efforts of the individual except through the regular organization of social life. The moral forces which women do so long to see applied to the uplifting of society will never be effective until women's wishes are translated into *power*. Their work will always be unfinished and ineffective until they become a part of the organized legislative machinery of society, just as they now are a part of its industrial organization. We need now, as never before, leaders of thought among women, organizers, women who

" See life steadily and see it whole."

Where are they? And will women be wise to recognize and follow them when they do appear?

www.ingramcontent.com/pod-product-compliance
Lightning Source LLC
Chambersburg PA
CBHW030900050726
47500CB00009B/539